'Who are  **)ered**
against h

'It doesn't matter,' she said through her swimming senses. 'I'm not real.'

'You are real now—in my arms.'

'Only here,' she whispered.

'The rest doesn't matter. Kiss me—kiss me.'

Julia did as he wanted, finding that after the years alone she still knew how. It was an intoxicating discovery. Now she allowed her hands and mouth to do as they pleased, and the things that pleased them were sensual, outrageous, experienced. He was right. This alone was real, and everything in her wanted to yield to it.

All the sensuality she normally kept banked down was flaming in his arms now, inciting him to explore her further, wanting more. He didn't know her real name, but her name no longer mattered. This woman was coming back to life, and he knew that he, and no other, must be the man to make that happen.

A FAMILY
FOR KEEPS

BY
LUCY GORDON

MILLS & BOON®

First published in Great Britain 2005
Harlequin Mills & Boon Limited,
Eton House, 18-24 Paradise Road, Richmond, Surrey TW9 1SR

© Lucy Gordon 2005

ISBN 0 263 84219 3

Set in Times Roman 10½ on 12 pt.
02-0305-45748

Printed and bound in Spain
by Litografía Rosés, S.A., Barcelona

PROLOGUE

THIS would be a good place to die.

She didn't utter the words but they were there in her heart. They swam up from the depths of the black water. They lingered around the cold grey stones and whispered away into the darkness.

She hadn't thought about dying when she'd planned to come here. Only revenge. There had been a long time to think about that.

The passion for revenge had brought her to this corner of Venice. She'd envisaged no further, certain that the next step would reveal itself when the time came.

Instead—nothing.

But what had she thought was going to happen when she got here? That the first face she saw would be the one she was seeking?

Or rather, one of the two faces she was seeking. One face she might not recognise after so many years, but the other she would know anywhere, any time. It haunted her by day and lived in her nightmares.

It was cold. The wind whistled along the canals and down the little alleys, and there was no comfort in all the world.

'I can't sleep at night, yet now I could sleep for ever. For ever—and ever—and ever—

'Yes, this would be a good place...'

CHAPTER ONE

AT MIDNIGHT Venice was the quietest city in the world, and in winter it could be the most mournful.

No cars, only the occasional sound of a passing boat, footsteps echoing on the hard stones, or the soft lap of tiny waves. And even this would soon die away into silence.

Here, by the Rialto Bridge, shadow merged with stone and stone with water, so that it was hard to tell if the bundle of clothes in the corner contained a living being or not.

At first sight, Piero thought that it probably did not, so still did it lie. He approached the bundle and gave it a tentative prod. It groaned softly, but didn't move. He frowned. A woman from the sound of it.

'Hey!' He tapped again and she rolled a little way so that he could discern a face. It was pale and drawn, and in this light that was all he could make out.

'Come with me,' he said in Italian.

For a moment she stared at him out of blank eyes, and he wondered if she had understood. Then she began to haul herself up, making no protest, asking no questions.

He half guided, half supported her away from the bridge, in to an alley, which turned into another alley and then into another, and another. To the casual eye they looked identical, all cold, narrow, gleaming with rain. But he found his way between them easily.

The woman with him barely noticed. Her heart was

like a frozen stone in her body, numbing all feeling except despair.

Once she stumbled and he held her safe, muttering, 'Not much farther.'

She could see now that they had reached the rear entrance of a building. There was just enough light to reveal that it was palatial. There was a large set of ornate double doors, maybe twelve feet high. But he passed these and led her to a much smaller door.

At first it stuck, but when he put his shoulder to it, with a movement that was half a push, half a shake, it yielded. Inside there was a torch, which he used to find the rest of the way.

Their footsteps sounded hollow on the tiled floors, giving her the sense of a grandiose building. She had a brief impression of a sweeping staircase and a wall with pale spaces where there had once been pictures.

A palace, but a shabby, abandoned palace.

At last he led her into a small room, where there were an armchair and a couple of sofas. Gently he guided her to one.

'Thank you,' she whispered, speaking for the first time.

He regarded her with surprise.

'English?' he asked.

She made the effort. '*Sì. Sono inglese.*'

'There's no need for that,' he said in perfect English. 'I speak your language. Now you must have some food. My name is Piero, by the way.'

When she hesitated he said, 'Any name will do— Cynthia, Anastasia, Wilhemina, Julia—'

'Julia,' she said. It was as good a name as any.

In one corner stood a tall ceramic stove, white with gilt decoration. In the lower part was a pair of doors, which he opened and began to pile wood inside.

'The electricity is off,' he explained, 'so it's lucky that the old stove remains. This one has stood here nearly two hundred years, and it still works. The trouble is I'm out of paper to light it.'

'Here. I got a newspaper on the plane.'

He showed no surprise at someone who had managed to buy a plane ticket and then slept in the street. He simply struck a match and in a few moments they had the beginnings of a fire.

At last they considered each other.

She saw an old man, tall, very thin, with a shock of white hair. He wore an ancient overcoat, tied with string around the waist, and a threadbare woollen scarf wrapped around his throat. He seemed a mixture of scarecrow and clown. His face was almost cadaverous, making his bright blue eyes exceptionally vivid by contrast. Even more noticeable was his smile, brilliant as a beacon, which flashed on and off.

Piero saw a woman whose age he couldn't guess except to put her in the mid thirties. Perhaps older, perhaps younger.

She was tall, and her figure, dressed in serviceable jeans, sweater and jacket, was a little too slim to be ideal. Her long fair hair hung forward like a curtain, making it hard to see her properly. Perhaps she preferred it that way because she mostly let it hang. Just once she brushed it aside, revealing that suffering had left her with a weary, troubled face, large eyes, and an air of distrusting all the world.

Her face was too lean and almost haggard. There was beauty there, but it came from a fire that burned far back behind her eyes.

'Thank you for finding me,' she said at last, speaking in a soft voice.

'You'd have been dead by morning, lying in that freezing place.'

'Probably.' She didn't sound as though this were of much interest. 'Where are we?'

'This is the Palazzo di Montese, home of the Counts di Montese for nine centuries. It's empty because the present count can't afford to live here.'

'So you live here instead?'

'That's right. And nobody bothers me because they're afraid of the ghost,' he added with relish.

'What ghost?'

He reached behind the chair to where an old sheet lay on the floor. Draping it over his head, he threw up his arms and began to wail.

'That ghost,' he said, tossing the sheet away and speaking normally.

She gave a faint smile. 'That's very scary,' she said.

He cackled like a delighted child. 'If people didn't believe in the ghost to start with they wouldn't take any notice of me. But everyone around here has heard about Annina, so they tell themselves it's her.'

'Who was she really?'

'She lived seven hundred years ago. She was a Venetian girl with a vast fortune but no title, which mattered a lot in those days. She fell madly in love with Count Ruggiero di Montese but he only married her for her money. When she'd borne him a son he locked her away. Eventually her body was found floating in the Grand Canal.

'Some said she was murdered, others that she had escaped in a small boat, which capsized. Now she's supposed to haunt this place. They say you can hear her voice calling up from the dungeons, begging to be released, crying to be allowed to see her child.'

He stopped because a faint sound had broken from her.

'Are you all right?' he asked, concerned.

'Yes,' she whispered.

'I haven't scared you, have I? Surely you don't believe in ghosts?'

'Not that kind of ghost,' Julia said softly.

He started the supper. By now the fire was burning merrily, so he fixed a grid over the burning wood, and used this to heat coffee.

'There's some sausages too,' he said. 'I cook them over the flames on forks. And I have rolls here. I have a friend with a restaurant, and he gives me yesterday's bread.'

When they were both settled and eating, she said, 'Why did you take me in? You know nothing about me.'

'I know that you needed help. What else is there to know?'

She understood. He had welcomed her into the fellowship of the dispossessed where nothing had to be told. The past did not exist.

So now she was officially a down-and-out. It was not such a bad thing to be. After the way she'd spent the last few years it might even be a step up.

'Here,' she said, reaching into a bag and bringing out a very small plastic bottle, containing red wine. 'The man next to me on the plane left it behind, so I took it.'

'Would it be indelicate to ask if you obtained the plane ticket in the same way?'

She gave a real smile then.

'Believe it or not, I didn't steal it,' she said. 'If you go to the right airline you can get a ticket from England to Venice for almost nothing. But when you get off the plane—' She shrugged.

'You can find winter prices in the hotels now,' Piero pointed out.

'Even so, I'm not spending a penny that I don't have to,' she said in a voice that was suddenly hard and stubborn. 'But I'll pay my way here,' she added.

'Cheaper than a hotel,' he agreed, waving a sausage.

'And the surroundings are grand. You can tell it's the real thing.'

'Know a bit about palaces, do you?'

'I've worked in a few,' she said cautiously. 'I'm surprised someone hasn't bought this to turn it into a luxury hotel.'

'They keep trying,' Piero said. 'But the owner won't sell. He could be a rich man, but it's been in his family for centuries, and he won't let it go.'

She rose and walked over to the tall window from which came some illumination, even though it was night. She understood why when she looked out and saw that the room overlooked the Grand Canal.

Even in late November, past midnight, this thoroughfare was busy with life. *Vaporetti*, the passenger boats, still plied their trade along the length of the canal, and lights shone on both banks.

In the room where she stood, beams of dim light coming through the stained glass windows made patterns on the tiled floor. These and the glow from the stove were the only defence against the darkness.

She didn't mind. The gloom of this place pleased her, where bright light would have been a torment.

'Do you live here all the time?' she asked Piero, sitting down and accepting another coffee from his hands.

'Yes, it's a good place. The amenities have been turned off, of course. No heat or lighting. But the pump outside still works, so we have fresh water. Let me show you.'

He led her down to the small stone outhouse where there was the pump and an earth closet.

'We even have a bathroom,' he declared with pride.

'Positively the lap of luxury,' she agreed solemnly.

When they went back inside she was suddenly swept by a weariness that almost knocked her off her feet. Piero looked at her with shrewd, kindly eyes.

'You're almost out of it, aren't you? You sleep on that sofa, and I'll have this one.'

He struck a theatrical attitude.

'Fair lady, do not fear to share a room with me. Be assured that I shall not molest you in your sleep. Or even out of it. That fire died years ago, and even in its better days it was never more than a modest flame.'

Julia could not help smiling at his droll manner.

'I wasn't afraid,' she assured him.

'No, I suppose certain things about me are fairly obvious,' said the gaunt scarecrow before her.

'I didn't mean that. I meant you've been kind and I know I can trust you.'

He gave a sigh.

'How I wish you were wrong!' he said mournfully. 'There are cushions over there, and here are some blankets. Sleep tight.'

She thanked him, curled up on the sofa in a blanket and was asleep in seconds. Piero was about to settle down for the night when a footstep outside alerted him, and a moment later a man entered, making him smile with pleasure.

'Vincenzo,' he said softly. 'It's good to see you again.'

The newcomer, who was in his late thirties with a lean, harsh face, asked, 'Why are we whispering?'

Piero pointed to the sofa, and Vincenzo nodded in understanding.

'Who is she?' he asked.

'She answers to Julia, and she's English. She's one of us.'

Vincenzo nodded, accepting the implication of 'us', and began to unpack two brown paper bags that he'd brought with him.

'A few leftovers from the restaurant,' he explained, bringing out some rolls, a carton of milk, and some slices of meat.

'Doesn't your boss mind you taking these?' Piero asked, claiming them with glee.

'Perks of the job. Besides, I can handle the boss.'

'That's very brave of you,' Piero said with a knowing wink. 'They say he's a terrible man.'

'So I've heard. Has anyone bothered you here?'

'Nobody ever does, although the owner is an even more terrible man. But if he tried to throw us out I expect you'd handle him too.'

Vincenzo grinned. 'I'd do my best.'

This was a game they played. Vincenzo was actually *il Conte di Montese*, the owner of the *palazzo* where they were standing, and also of the restaurant where he worked. Piero knew this. Vincenzo knew that he knew it, and Piero knew that Vincenzo knew he knew. But it suited them both for it to remain unspoken between them.

On the sofa Julia stirred and muttered. Vincenzo moved a little closer and sat down, watching her.

'How did you find her?' he asked quietly.

'Curled up in a corner of an alley, which is odd because she says she flew here.'

'She took so much trouble to come to Venice, only to collapse in the street?' Vincenzo mused. 'What the devil is driving her?'

'Perhaps she'll tell me the reason later,' Piero said. 'But not if I ask.'

Vincenzo nodded, understanding the code by which Piero and those like him lived. He was used to dropping into his empty home to find various squatters sheltering there.

He knew that a sensible man would have driven them out, but, despite his grim aspect, he lacked the heart. He looked in occasionally to keep an eye on the place, but he'd found that Piero was better than any caretaker, and the building was safe with him. Now his visits were as much to check on the old man's welfare as for any other reason.

Julia stirred again, settling into a position where more of her face was visible.

Moving quietly, Vincenzo dropped to his knees beside her and studied her. He supposed he shouldn't be doing that while she was unknowing and defenceless, but something about her drew him so that he could not turn away.

Her face spoke of mysteries and denied them in the same moment. She wasn't a girl, he thought, probably somewhere in her thirties, marked by grief and with a withdrawn look so intense that it was there even in sleep.

Her mouth was wide, generous, designed to be mobile and expressive. He had known women with lips like that. They laughed easily, talked well, and kissed urgently with warm, sweet breath.

But this woman looked as if she seldom smiled, except as a polite mask. And she had forgotten how to kiss. She had forgotten love and pleasure and happiness. This was a face from which tenderness had been driven by sheer force. Its owner was capable of anything.

But it hadn't always been true. She had started life differently. Traces of vulnerability were still there, although perhaps not for long. Something had brought her to the point where life would harden her quickly.

Then a strange feeling came over him, as though the very air had moved, and the ground beneath him had trembled. He blinked, shaking his head, and the feeling vanished. Quickly he moved away.

'What's the matter?' Piero asked, handing him a cup of coffee.

'Nothing. It's just that for a moment I felt I'd seen her before. But where—?' He sighed. 'I must be imagining it.'

He drank his coffee and turned to go. At the door he stopped and handed Piero some money.

'Look after her,' he said quietly.

When Vincenzo had gone Piero wrapped himself in a blanket and lay down on the other sofa. After a while he slept.

Doors clanged again and again. It was a dreadful, hollow sound, and it soon became agonising.

She flung herself against one of those iron doors, pounding and shrieking that she should not be here. But there was no response, no help. Only stony, cold indifference.

There were bars at the windows. She pulled herself up to them, looking through at the world from which she was shut out.

She could see a wedding. It did not seem strange to find such a scene in this dreary place, for she knew instinctively that they were connected.

There was the groom, young and handsome, smiling on his day of triumph. Was there something about his smile that wasn't quite right, as though he was far from being the man his bride thought?

She knew nothing of that. The poor little fool thought he loved her. She was young, innocent, and stupid.

Here she came, glowing with love triumphant. Julia gripped the bars in horror as that naïve girl threw back her veil, revealing the face beneath—

Her own face.

'Don't,' she said hoarsely. 'Don't do it. Don't marry him, *for pity's sake don't marry him.*'

The last words were a scream, and suddenly she was sitting up, tortured into wakefulness, tears streaming down her face, and Piero kneeling beside her, his arms about her, trying vainly to offer comfort for a wrong that could never be put right.

For breakfast next morning Piero laid on a feast.

'Where did these come from?' Julia asked, looking at the rolls stuffed with meat.

'From my friend from the restaurant who dropped in last night, the one I told you about.'

'He sounds like a really good friend. Is he one of us?'

'In what sense?'

'You know—stranded.'

'Well, he's got a roof over his head, but you might call him stranded in other ways. He's lost everyone he ever loved.'

Over breakfast she produced some money. 'It's only a little but it might help. You'll know where the bargains are.'

'Splendid. We'll go out together.'

She wrapped up thickly and followed him out into the day. He led her through a labyrinth of tiny *calles*, until her head was swimming. How could anyone find their way around this place?

Suddenly they were in the open, and the Rialto Bridge

reared up over them, straight ahead. She'd been here the night before and gone to frozen sleep at one end, where the shore railings curved towards the water.

She'd come to this place searching for someone…

Now she looked around, but all the faces seemed to converge, making her giddy. And perhaps *he* had never been here after all.

Venice was bustling with life. Barges made their way through the canals, stopping to seize the bags of rubbish that had been dumped by the water's edge. More barges, filled with supplies, arrived at the open air market at the base of the Rialto.

Piero stocked up with fiendish efficiency, buying more produce with less money than she would have thought possible.

'That's a good morning's work,' he said. 'Now we—you're shivering. I guess you took a chill from those stones last night. Let's get you into the warm.'

She tried to smile but she was feeling worse by the minute, and was glad to turn back.

When they reached home Piero tended her like a mother, building up the stove and making her some hot coffee.

'You've got a nasty cold there,' he said when she started to cough.

'Yes,' she snuffled miserably.

'I've got to go out for a while. Stay close to the stove while I'm gone.'

He left quickly, and she was alone in the rapidly darkening building. There was something blessed in the silence.

She went to the window overlooking the Grand Canal. Just outside was a tiny garden, bordered by tall wrought iron railings, right next to the water.

By craning her neck she could make out the Rialto Bridge, and the bank lined with outdoor tables on the far side of the canal. The cafés were filled with people, determined not to be put off by the time of year.

She wandered back to the stove and sat on the floor, beside it, dozing on and off.

Then something made her eyes open sharply. The last of the light had gone, and she could hear footsteps in the corridor. It didn't sound like Piero, but somebody younger.

The sound drew close and halted. Then the door handle turned. It was enough to make her leap up and hurry into the shadows where the intruder could not see her. Inwardly she was screaming, *Go away! Leave me alone!*

She stood still, her heart thumping wildly, as the door opened and a man came in. He set the bag he was carrying on the floor, and looked around as though expecting to see somebody.

She told herself not to be foolish. This was probably Piero's friend. But still she couldn't make herself move. Nobody was a friend to her.

The man came into a shaft of light from a large window. It was soft, almost gloomy light, but she could make out that he was tall, with a rangy build and a lean face that suggested a man in his thirties.

Suddenly he grew alert, as though realising that he was not alone. 'Who is it?' he called, looking around.

She tried to force herself to speak, but a frozen hand seemed to be grasping her throat.

'I know you're somewhere,' he said. 'There's no need to hide from me.'

Then he moved quickly, pulling back one of the long curtains that hung beside the window, revealing her, pressed against the wall, eyes wide with dread and hostility.

'*Dio Mio!*' he exclaimed. 'A ghost.'

He put out his hand and would have laid it on her shoulder, but she flinched away.

'Don't touch me,' she said hoarsely in English.

His hand fell at once.

'I'm sorry,' he replied, also in English. 'Don't be afraid of me. Why are you hiding?'

'I'm—not—hiding,' she said with an effort, knowing she sounded crazy. 'I just—didn't know who you were.'

'My name is Vincenzo, a friend of Piero's. I was here last night but you were asleep.'

'He told me about you,' she said jerkily, 'but I wasn't sure—'

'I'm sorry if I startled you.'

He was talking gently, soothing her as he would have done a wild animal, and gradually she felt her irrational fear subside.

'I heard you coming,' she said, 'and—' A fit of coughing drowned the rest.

'Come into the warm,' Vincenzo said, beckoning her to the stove.

When she still hesitated he took hold of her hands. His own hands were warm and powerful, and they drew her forward irresistibly.

He eased her down onto the sofa, but instead of releasing her he slid his hands up her arms and grasped her, not roughly but with a strength that felt like protection.

'Piero says your name is Julia.'

She hesitated for a split second. 'Yes, that's right. Julia.'

'Why are you trembling?' he asked. 'It can't be that bad.'

Something in those words broke her control and she shuddered violently.

'It is that bad,' she said, in a hoarse voice. 'Everything is that bad. It always will be. It's like a maze. I keep thinking that there must be a way out, but there isn't. Not after all this time. It's too late, I know it's too late, and if I had any sense I'd go away and forget, but I *can't* forget.'

'Julia.' He gave her a little shake. *'Julia.'*

She didn't hear him. She was beyond anything he could say or do to reach her. Words poured out of her unstoppably, while tears slid down her face.

'You can't get rid of ghosts,' she wept, 'just by telling them to go, because they're everywhere, before you and behind you and most of all *inside* you.'

'Yes, I know,' he murmured grimly, but she rushed on, unheeding.

'I have to do it. I can't stop and I won't, and I can't help who gets hurt, don't you see that?'

'I'm afraid the person who gets hurt will be you,' he said.

For answer she grasped him back, digging her fingers into him painfully.

'It doesn't matter,' she said. 'Nobody can hurt me any more. When you've reached your limit, you're safe, so I don't have to worry, and there's nothing to stop me doing what I have to.'

Abruptly she released him and buried her face in her hands as the feverish energy that had briefly sustained her drained away, leaving her weak and shaking.

For a moment Vincenzo was nonplussed. Then he put his arms right around her and held her in a tight clasp.

He didn't try to speak, knowing that there was nothing to say, but his grip was rough and fierce, silently telling her she was not alone.

After a long time he felt her relax, although even that had a strained quality, as though she had forced it to happen.

'I'm all right,' she said in a muffled voice.

He relaxed his grip and drew back slightly. 'Are you sure?'

'I'm all right,' she insisted fiercely. 'I'm all right, I'm all right.'

'I just want to help you.'

'I don't need anyone's help!'

Instantly he got to his feet and stepped back.

'I'm sorry,' she said, 'I didn't mean to be rude, it's just—'

'You don't have to explain. I know how it is.'

She looked up at him, and in the dim light he had an impression of a pale face, surrounded by long fair hair, like one of the other-worldly creatures that populated the pictures that had once filled this palace. He had grown up with the ghostly faces, accepting them as a normal part of his world. It startled him to meet one in reality.

'It's like that for you too?' she asked.

After a moment's pause he said, 'For everyone in one way or another. Some less—some more.'

He said the last words hoping she would tell him about herself, but he could see her defences being hastily reassembled. The moment was already slipping away, and when he heard the sound of Piero approaching he knew it had gone.

CHAPTER TWO

PIERO pushed open the door, his face brightening when he saw the visitor.

'*Ciao,*' Vincenzo said, clapping him on the shoulder.

'*Ciao,*' Piero said, looking around. 'Ah, you two have met.'

'Yes, I'm afraid I gave the *signorina* a fright.'

'Why so formal? This isn't a *signorina*. It's Julia.'

'Or are you perhaps a *signora*?' Vincenzo queried. 'You understand, a *signora* is—?'

'Yes, thank you, I speak Italian,' she said edgily. 'A *signora* is a married woman. I'm a *signorina*.'

She wasn't sure why she insisted on parading her knowledge of Italian at that moment, unless it was pride. Vincenzo's understanding had made her defensive.

'So you speak my language,' Vincenzo said. 'I congratulate you. So often the English won't trouble to learn other languages. Do you speak it well?'

'I'm not sure. I haven't used it for a while. I'm out of practice. I can brush up on it here.'

'Not as easily as you think. In Venice we speak Venetian.'

After that he dived into the bags he'd brought, seeming to forget her, which was a relief. She took the chance to wander away to the window and stand with her back to them, watching the canal, but not seeing it.

Instead she saw Vincenzo in her mind's eye, trying to understand the darkness she sensed, in his looks and in the man himself. Everything about him was dark, from

22

his black hair to his deep brown eyes. Even his wide mouth, with its tendency to quirk wryly, suggested that he was not really amused. Or, if so, that the humour was bleak and fit only for the gallows.

A man whose inner world was as grim and haunted as her own.

But still she tried to thrust him from her mind. He was dangerous because he saw too much, tricking her into blurting out thoughts that had been rioting in her head, but which she'd kept rigidly repressed.

I have to do it—I can't help who gets hurt.

Say nothing. Never let them suspect what you're planning. Smile, hate, and protect your secrets.

That was how she had lived.

And in one moment he had triggered an avalanche, luring her into a dangerous admission.

Nobody can hurt me any more—so there's nothing to stop me doing what I have to.

She looked around, and saw to her relief that Vincenzo had gone. She hadn't heard him leave.

Piero was beaming at her, waving a bread roll in invitation.

'We feast like kings,' he announced grandiloquently. 'Sit down and let me serve you the Choice of the Day. Trust me, I was once the head chef at the Paris Ritz.'

She wasn't sure what to believe. Unlikely as it sounded, it might just be true.

Her cold grew worse over the next few days. Piero's care never failed her. From some store room he managed to produce a bed. It was old, shabby and needed propping up in one corner, but it was more comfortable than her sofa, and she fell onto it blissfully.

But he refused to let her thank him.

'It comes easily to me,' he assured her. 'I used to be a top physician at Milan's largest hospital.'

'As well as being a great chef?' she teased him.

He gave her a reproachful look. 'That was the other night.'

'I'm sorry. I should have thought.'

She knew that Vincenzo sometimes came to visit, but she always lay still, feigning sleep. She did not want to talk to him. He threatened secrets that she must keep.

But he too had painful secrets. He'd hinted as much.

Every second afternoon Piero would go out, returning three hours later. He never told her where he went, and she guessed that these occasions were connected with the events that had brought him to this limbo.

One afternoon he entered wearing his usual cheerful look, which became even brighter when he saw her.

'Did you find what you were looking for?' she ventured.

'Not today. She wasn't there, but she will be one day.'

'She?'

'Elena, my daughter. Ah, coffee! Splendid!'

She respected his desire to change the subject, but later, when the darkness had fallen, she asked gently,

'Where is Elena now?'

He was silent for so long she was afraid he was offended, but then he said, 'It's hard to explain. We sort of—mislaid each other. But she's worked abroad a great deal, and I've always been there to meet her when she returned. Always the same place, at San Zaccaria—that's the landing stage where the boats come in near St Mark's. If I'm not there she'll want to know why, so I mustn't let her down. I just have to be patient, you see.'

'Yes,' she said sadly. 'I see.'

She wrapped the blanket around her and settled down,

hoping that soon her mind would start working properly again, and she would know what to do next.

Then she wondered if that would ever happen, for when she closed her eyes the old pictures began to play back, and there was only grief, misery, despair, followed by rage and bitterness, so that soon she was hammering on the door again, screaming for a release that would never come.

Sometimes she would surface from her fever to find Vincenzo there, then go back to sleep, curiously contented. This was becoming her new reality, and when she awoke once to find Vincenzo gone she knew an odd sense of disturbance. But then she saw Piero, and relaxed again.

He came over and felt her forehead, pursing his lips to show that he wasn't pleased with what he found.

'I got you something,' he said, dissolving a powder in hot water. 'It'll make you feel better.'

'Thanks, Piero,' she said hoarsely. 'Or do I mean Harlequin?'

'What's that?'

'Harlequin, Columbine, Pierrot, Pierrette,' she said vaguely. 'They're all characters from the Commedia dell'Arte. Pierrot's a clown, isn't he?'

His eyes were very bright. 'It's as good a name as any. Like Julia.'

'Yes,' she agreed.

The cold remedy drink made her feel better and she got to her feet, rubbing her eyes. Her throat and her forehead were still hot, but she was determined to get up, if only for a while.

It was mid-afternoon and since the light was good she

went out of the little room into the great reception hall
and began to look about her.

The pictures might be gone but the frescoes painted
directly onto the walls were still here. She studied them,
until she came to one that stopped her in her tracks as
though it had spoken to her.

It was at the top of the stairs, and showed a woman
with long fair hair flying wildly around her face like a
mad halo. Her eyes were large and distraught as though
with some ghastly vision. She had been to hell, and now
she would never really escape.

'That's Annina,' said Piero, who had followed her.

'It's Annina if we want to be fanciful,' said Vincenzo's
voice.

He had come in silently and watched them for a moment before speaking.

'What do you mean, "fanciful"?' she asked.

He came up the stairs, closer to her. She watched him
with hostile eyes, angry with herself for being glad to see
him.

'We don't know if that's what she really looked like,'
he explained. 'This was done a couple of centuries later,
by an artist who played up the drama for all it was worth.

'See, there are prison bars in one corner, and there's a
child over here. And this man, with the demonic face, is
Annina's husband. Count Francesco, his direct descen-
dant, didn't like having the family scandal revived. He
even wanted the artist to paint over it.'

Scandalised, Julia spoke without thinking. 'Paint over
a Correggio?'

She could have cut her tongue out the next moment.
Vincenzo's raised eyebrows showed that he fully appre-
ciated what she'd revealed.

'Well done,' he said. 'It *is* Correggio. And of course

he refused to cover it. Then people began to admire it, and Francesco, who was as big a philistine as Correggio said he was, realised that it must be good after all. So it's stayed here, and people take their view of the story from this very melodramatic picture. Naturally, the ghost looks just like her. Ask Piero.'

His smile showed that he knew exactly the trick the old man was playing to scare off intruders.

'I'm sure I don't know what she looks like,' Piero said loftily. 'I've never seen her.'

'But she's been heard often,' Vincenzo observed. He clapped Piero on the shoulder. 'I've left a few things for you. I may see you later.' He pointed a commanding finger at Julia. 'You—into the warm, right now.'

She returned to the little room with relief. Her brief expedition had lowered her strength, and when she had eaten something she curled up again and was soon asleep.

It was after midnight when Vincenzo reappeared. When he was settled he became sunk in thought. 'How many people,' he asked at last, 'could identify a Correggio at once?'

'Not many,' Piero conceded.

'That's what I thought.' He glanced at the sleeping Julia. 'Has she told you anything about herself?'

'No, but why should she? Our kind respect each other's privacy. You know that.'

'Yes, but there's something about her that worries me. It could be risky to leave her too much alone.'

'But suppose she wants to be left alone?'

'I think she does,' Vincenzo mused, remembering the desperation with which she had cried, 'I don't need any-one's help.'

Nobody said it like that unless their need for help was terrible.

All his life he'd had an instinctive affinity with needy creatures. When his father had bought him a puppy he'd chosen the runt of the litter, the one who had held back timidly. His father had been displeased, but the boy, stubborn beneath his quiet manner, had said, 'This one,' and refused to budge.

After that there had been his sister, his twin, discounted by their parents as a mere girl, and therefore loved by him the more. They had been close all their lives until she had cruelly repaid his devotion by dying, and leaving him bereft.

He had loved a woman, refusing to see her grasping nature, until she'd callously abandoned him.

Now he would have said that his days of opening his heart to people were over. No man could afford to be like that, and he'd developed armour in self-defence.

He made an exception for Piero, whom he'd known in better days. There was something about the old man's gentle madness, his humour in the face of misfortune, that called to him despite his resolutions.

As for the awkward, half-hostile woman he'd found sleeping here, he couldn't imagine why he'd allowed her to stay. Perhaps because she wanted nothing from him, and seemed consumed by a bitterness that matched his own.

Suddenly a long sigh came from the bed. As they watched she threw back the blanket and eased her legs over the side.

Vincenzo tensed, about to speak to her, but then something in her demeanour alerted him and he stopped. She stood for a moment, staring into the distance with eyes that were vague. Slowly Vincenzo got to his feet and went to stand before her.

'Julia,' he said softly.

She made no response and he realised that she was still asleep. When he spoke her name she did not see or hear him. After a moment she turned away and began to walk slowly to the door.

She seemed to know her way as well in the darkness and in the light. Without stumbling she opened the door, and went out into the main hall.

At the foot of the stairs she stopped, remaining still for a long time. Moonlight, streaming through the windows, showed her shrouded in a soft blue glow, like a phantom. She raised her head so that her long hair fell back and they could both see that her eyes were fixed on the picture of Annina, at the top of the stairs.

'Can she see it?' Piero muttered.

'It's the only thing she *can* see,' Vincenzo told him. 'Nothing else exists for her.'

She began to move again, slowly setting one foot in front of the other, climbing the broad stairs.

'Stop her,' Piero said urgently.

Vincenzo shook his head. 'This is her decision. We can't interfere.'

Moving quietly, he began to follow her up the stairs until she came to a halt in front of the fresco showing the distraught Annina. It too lay in the path of the moonlight that entered through windows high up in the hall.

'Julia,' Vincenzo said again, speaking very quietly.

Silence. She was not aware of him.

'Dammit, that's not her real name,' Vincenzo said frantically. 'How can I reach her with it?'

'There's another name you might try,' Piero murmured.

Vincenzo shot him an uneasy glance. 'Don't talk like that, Piero. Enough of superstition.'

'Is it superstition?'

'You know as well as I do that the dead don't come back.'

'Then who is she?'

Vincenzo didn't reply. He couldn't.

A soft moan broke from her. She was reaching up to touch the picture, beginning to talk in soft, anguished tones.

'I loved him, and he shut me away—for years—until I died—I died—'

'Julia,' Vincenzo said, knowing it would be useless.

Instead of answering she began to thump the wall.

'I died—' she screamed. 'Just as he meant me to. *My baby—my baby—*'

Abruptly all the strength went out of her and she leaned against the wall. Vincenzo grasped her gently and drew her away.

'It's all right,' he said. 'I'm here. Don't give in. Stay strong whatever you do.'

She looked up at him out of despairing eyes, and he knew that she couldn't see him. For her, he didn't exist.

'Let's go,' he said.

She shook her head and tried to pull away. 'I must find him,' she said hoarsely. 'Don't you understand?'

'Of course, but not tonight. Get some rest, and later I'll help you find him.'

'You can't help me. Nobody can.'

'But I will,' he insisted. 'There has to be a way if there's a friend to help you. And you have a friend now.'

Whether she understood the words or whether it was his tone that reached her, she stopped struggling and stood passive.

It was the first time he'd seen her face turned towards him without suspicion or defensiveness. But he could still feel her trembling, and it made him do something on impulse.

Putting his hands on either side of her face, he kissed her softly again and again, her eyes, her cheeks, her mouth.

'It's all right,' he said again. 'I'm here.'

She did not reply, but her eyes closed. He wrapped his arms right around her, leading her carefully down the stairs. She held onto him, eyes still closed, but moving with confidence while he was there.

Step by step they made their way to the bottom of the stairs, then back into the little room, where Vincenzo guided her to the bed so that she could lie down again.

She murmured something that he could not catch, then seemed to relax all at once. Vincenzo pulled the blanket up and tucked it tenderly around her.

'Not a word of this, my friend,' he said, joining Piero. 'Not to anyone else and especially not to her.'

Piero nodded. 'We wait until she mentions it.'

'If she ever does.'

'You think she won't remember what happened tonight?'

'I don't think she even knows what happened tonight. She wasn't here.'

'Then where was she?'

'In some far place where nobody else is invited. It's dark and fearful, and it's from there that she draws her strength.'

'Her head must be very muddled if she thinks she's Annina.' Piero sighed. 'It was like meeting a ghost in the flesh.'

Vincenzo raised an eyebrow. 'Rid yourself of that idea, my friend. She is no ghost.'

'But you heard what she said. She was buried—she died—the child—she was speaking as Annina.'

'No,' Vincenzo said sombrely. 'What's really horrifying is that she was speaking as herself.'

At last Julia awoke to find everything clear. Her body was cool again and the inside of her head was orderly.

'Have you come back to us?'

Looking around, she saw Vincenzo sitting nearby, and wondered how long he'd been there.

'Yes, I think I have,' she said. 'More or less. I may even be in one piece.'

She swung her legs gingerly to the floor and began to ease herself up. He crossed the floor quickly and held out a hand.

'Steady,' he said as she clung to him. 'You haven't been eating enough to keep a mouse alive. No wonder you're weak.'

'I'm not weak. You can let me go.'

He did so and she promptly sat down again.

'OK, I'm weak.'

'Give yourself time. Don't rush it.'

He spoke in his normal way, but she had an odd sensation that something was different. He was looking at her curiously, with a question in his eyes.

'What's the matter?' she asked.

'How do you mean?'

'You're giving me a strange look.'

For once she seemed to have caught him off guard. 'I was just—wondering if you're really better. You certainly seem—' He seemed to be searching for the right words. 'You seem more like your normal self.'

'That's how I feel,' she said, wondering what he was implying.

'Good,' he said, sounding deflated. 'Stay there while I make you some soup.'

The hot soup was straight from heaven. When she'd eaten she went down to the pump for a wash.

She returned to find Vincenzo still there. He was sitting by the window, sunk in his own thoughts, and didn't at first hear her. When she hailed him he seemed to come out of a dream.

'OK?'

'Yes. Who'd have thought washing in freezing water could feel so good? How long was I out of it?'

'Just over a week.'

'I slept for a week?'

'Not all the time. You kept recovering slightly, then you'd insist on getting up and walking around before you were ready. So you got worse again.'

'But to sleep for a week!'

'Or a hundred years,' he said ironically.

'Yes, now I know how the sleeping princess felt. I've even lost track of the date. Mind you, I often—'

She checked, as if about to reveal something, but then thinking better of it. Vincenzo's curiosity was heightened.

'You often forget the date?' he asked. 'How come?'

'Nothing. I didn't mean that.'

She met his gaze, defying him to disbelieve her openly, although she knew he wasn't convinced. He backed down first.

'Well, anyway, it's December second,' he said.

'That's weird, to fall asleep in one month and awake in another. And no newspapers or television. It's strange how nice life can be without them.'

'To shut the world out!' he mused. 'Yes, that would be nice. What is it?'

He asked because she had suddenly stopped in the middle of the floor, and her eyes became vague, as though she were listening to distant voices.

'I don't know,' she said. 'It's just that—I had such dreams—such dreams—'

'Can you recall any of them?' Nobody could have told from Vincenzo's voice that the answer mattered to him.

'I think so—there was—there was—'

She closed her eyes, fighting desperately to summon back a memory that lay just beyond reach. It was disturbing, and yet in its heart lay a feeling of peace, the very one she was seeking.

'Try,' Vincenzo said, unable to keep a hint of urgency out of his voice.

But it was a fatal thing to say. The minute she reached out for the dream it vanished.

'It's gone,' she said with a sigh. 'I hope it comes back. I think it was lovely.'

He shrugged. 'If you can't remember it, how do you know it was lovely?'

'You know how it is with dreams. They leave you with a kind of feeling, even when you forget the details.'

'And what feeling did this one leave behind?'

'It was peaceful and—happy—' She said the last word in a tone of astonishment. 'Oh, heck, it was probably nothing at all.'

'Nothing at all,' Vincenzo agreed.

She looked around. 'Where's Piero?'

'He's gone to the landing stage.'

'Looking for Elena? Perhaps she'll come today.'

Vincenzo shook his head. 'She'll never come. She died several years ago.'

Julia sighed. 'I wondered about that. I can't make him out. How does he come to be living like this?'

'At one time he was a university professor. Elena, his daughter, was everything to him, especially after his wife died. Then she died too and everything finished for him.'

'He lost a child?' she murmured.

She felt something tearing at her at the thought of Piero and his lost child. There was no pain like it. How could anyone recover?

'She was drowned while out sailing. They found her body three days later. I was on the quay when they brought her home, and I saw Piero, staring out to sea as the boat came in. But when it landed he didn't seem to see it, just walked away. He didn't even go to her funeral because he refused to believe she was dead.

'He's never accepted it. I've tried to make him understand. I've even taken him to the cemetery at San Michele, to show him her grave, but he won't look at it.'

'Of course not. You shouldn't have done that.'

'Isn't it better for him to face reality?'

'Why?' she asked quickly. 'What's so marvellous about reality?'

'Nothing, I suppose.'

'Let him cling to his hope. Without it he'd go crazy.'

'But he's already a little crazy.'

'Then let him be crazy, if that's the only way to stop his heart breaking,' Julia said, almost pleading with him. 'How can you understand?'

'Perhaps I can,' he said wryly. 'Anyway, I know what you mean. Tell me—are you crazy?'

'Oh, yes,' she said, almost cheerfully. 'I'm as mad as a hatter.'

'Because of the ghosts inside you? That's what you said.'

'If I did, I was feverish. I don't remember.'

'I think you do. I think you remember what you want to remember.'

Her relaxed mood vanished and his probing made her nerves taut again.

'I don't know who you are,' she said in a low, angry voice, 'but I can't see why you come here.'

'Must there be a reason?'

'Well, you don't need a place to sleep, do you? And why else would you be here except to patronise us? No, I'm sorry—' She threw up her hand. 'I didn't mean to say that. But just don't start getting clever with me.'

'Not even to stop you hurting someone?'

'I'm not going to hurt anyone.'

'Except yourself.'

'That's my problem.'

'*Mio Dio*, it's like trying to argue with a hornet. I only said you picked your memories to suit yourself.'

She gave an edgy laugh.

'If I could do that I'd forget a lot of things. It's the ones I can't help remembering that are the problem. Piero's the wise one. He's found a way to choose what to remember.'

'Yes, I guess he has,' Vincenzo said wryly. 'And I think I hear him coming, so can we delay our hostilities for another time?'

She walked over to the window, annoyed with herself. For a brief moment she had been at ease with him, regaining human feelings that she had thought lost for ever. Then he had stepped over an invisible line, actually daring to understand her. And he had become an enemy again.

The door opened and Piero appeared.

'Not today?' Julia asked sympathetically.

'Not today,' he said brightly. 'Never mind. Maybe next time.'

Abruptly Vincenzo remembered that he had to be somewhere else, clapped Piero on the shoulder, and departed.

CHAPTER THREE

THE next afternoon, while Piero was out, Julia spent the time looking around the great building. The sight was both melancholy and magnificent.

The grandeur was still there. The Counts di Montese had lived like kings, secure in their wealth and authority. Now it was all gone. The rooms were silent and draughts whispered down the corridors.

The walls of the grand staircase were lined with frescoes, leading to a large one at the top, that she now knew was Annina. Watching it gave her a vague sensation of disturbance that grew with every moment. She wanted to run away, but she forced herself to keep climbing until she was facing the painted woman with her wild hair and her tormented eyes. Her heart raced faster and faster; she was suffocating—

And then it stopped. As suddenly as it had started the suffocating misery and terror ceased, leaving her with a feeling of calm release, almost as though someone had laid a comforting hand on her, and said, 'I'm here. I'll make it all right.'

The sensation was so clear that she looked around to see who had spoken. It was almost a surprise to find herself alone, the awareness of another presence was so intense.

She moved away from the picture. The disturbing currents that had flowed from it a moment ago had vanished. Now it was just a picture again.

Walking on through the building, she explored the

rooms that were almost bare of furniture. She grew more fascinated as she went from room to room. She knew and understood places like this.

She took her time, studying the frescoes on the ceilings, some of which were very fine. Unlike the pictures, they were fixed, impossible to sell without tearing down the building. They gave her an idea of how magnificent this place must have been at its height.

At last she went into the great bedroom where the Count di Montese must have lived and held court. It was empty except for the huge bed and a few chairs, but the sense of grandeur lingered. She looked up at the ceiling frescoes. Then she tensed.

Was it her imagination, or was there a patch where the colours were darker? The afternoon light was fading fast, and she could not be sure.

Hurriedly she found a chair, pulled it out and reached up. By standing on tiptoe she could just touch the patch and feel that it was damp.

And that meant it was recent, she thought. Somehow water was coming through that ceiling right now.

But where did it come from? She ran to the window and pushed it open, leaning out to look up. Just above her was a row of small windows, suggesting an attic.

She hurried out and down the corridor, urgently seeking a way of getting up to the next floor. At last she found a small, plain door that looked as if it might be the one. But it was locked.

There was no time to lose. She was assailed by a vision of water pouring down through ceilings, over walls, unstoppably ruining the beautiful building.

She rattled the door, which was old and shaky on its hinges. There was only one way to do this. Gathering all the strength she could muster, she gave a hard kick, and knew an unbelievable sense of satisfaction when the door gave way.

Oh, the blissful release of one violent action!

She sprinted up the stairs and found herself in the great attic at the top of the building.

It was long and low, and seemed to be used as a store room. There was some furniture here, and what looked like pictures, wrapped in heavy brown paper.

And there, by the wall, was a water tank, with a pipe leading from it across the floor. The pipe was old and broken, and water was pouring from it with terrible inevitability. If not stopped it would flood the floor, soaking down until the whole building was damaged.

Then she set her chin.

'Not if I have anything to do with it!' she breathed.

She needed something to wrap around the pipe! But what? Rags would do for now.

A frantic search around the attic revealed nothing of any use, and the water was pooling across the floor, threatening the wrapped pictures that were leaning against the wall.

Her handkerchief was too small. She would have to use her woollen sweater. Wrenching it off, she wound it frantically around the belching pipe, but already water was seeping through.

Something else! Her shirt. She managed to tear this into strips and tie them around the pipe, but the water just kept coming. Soon she would need a torch, as the light was fading every moment.

She must dash downstairs to find something more reliable, and put more clothes on, since with both her sweater and shirt gone she was freezing in her bra. She headed for the door, but stopped to rush back to the pipe and tighten the rough bandage. Then she raced back to the door, not looking where she was going, and colliding with someone.

At once two strong arms went around her and she fell to the floor with her assailant.

With everything in her she cursed him. It was hard when she was out of breath, but she did her best. She cursed him for delaying her, she cursed him for lying on top of her so that she couldn't escape the sensation of his big, powerful body against hers. She cursed him for his warm breath on her face and the smell of lemons and olives that came from him. Above all she cursed him for the feel of his loins against hers, and the sweet warmth that was beginning deep inside. She rejected it, she repudiated it, she wanted no part of it. But it was there, and it was all his fault.

'Get off me,' she snapped.

As he recognised her voice Vincenzo demanded, 'What the devil—?'

'Get off me.'

For a moment he didn't move. He might have been too thunderstruck to move, lying against her, gasping.

She too was gasping, she realised in outrage. The warmth was becoming heat, spreading through her.

'I said get off me.'

He did so, moving slowly, as if caught in a dream. In the gloom he pulled her to her feet, but didn't release her. Looking into his eyes she saw her own sensations mirrored and, perversely, it increased her rage at him.

'What are you doing up here?' he asked with difficulty.

'Trying to stop the place from being wrecked. There's a burst water pipe up here, and it's going to flood this building from the top down.'

He seemed dazed. 'What—what did you say?'

She ground her teeth. Was the house going to be ruined because he couldn't take in more than one idea at a time?

Then she saw that his gaze was riveted on her, and in the same moment she realised that her bra had become undone in the struggle, slipping down, revealing her full, generous breasts. Furiously she wrenched herself from his grasp, snapping, 'Can I have your attention please?'

'You've got that,' he said distractedly.

'Just you mind your manners.'

That seemed to pull him back to reality.

'I'm sorry, it must have happened when—it was an accident—'

'An accident that wouldn't have happened if you hadn't jumped me.'

'Well, I wasn't expecting to find you here in a state of undress. *Mio Dio*, you haven't brought a man up here, have you?'

'There's going to be another accident if you don't watch it,' she threatened. 'One that may leave you unable to walk. Do I make myself clear?'

'Perfectly.'

She had been trying to hook up her bra at the back, but she was too angry to concentrate and it wasn't working.

'Can I help you?' he asked.

'No funny business.'

'That's a promise. I'll count myself lucky to get out of here alive.'

She turned and stood there while he hooked up the ends, his fingers brushing softly against her skin. She braced herself against the sensation on her skin that was already overheated from something that had nothing to do with the winter temperature.

When he'd finished he said meekly, 'Am I allowed to

ask what you're doing here without being threatened with bodily violence?'

She remembered the broken pipe. In the last few minutes it had receded into unreality.

'You've got a burst pipe up here,' she said. 'It could soak the whole place.'

She led him across the floor to where he could see better. As he realised the danger, a violent word, sounding like a curse, burst from him.

He stripped off his scarf and wound it around the pipe. But it too was instantly soaked.

'Hold it,' he told her tersely. 'I'm going to get something safer.'

He stopped just long enough to pull off his jacket and put it about her shoulders. Then he made a run for it.

Julia shrugged her arms into the jacket, which was blessedly warm. She was deeply shaken by the last few minutes.

She'd had it all sussed—or so she'd thought. No hopes, no pity, no sympathy, and above all no feelings, *of any kind*.

But some feelings were harder to suppress than others. They acted independently of thought and anger, and left a trail of problems.

She set her chin. Problems were made to be overcome.

In a few minutes Vincenzo was back, bearing a roll of heavy, sticky tape.

'This will hold it for a while,' he said, winding it around the pipe and the wadding. 'But we need a plumber.'

He took out his cell phone and dialled. There followed a curt conversation in Venetian.

'There'll be someone here in about half an hour,' he

said, switching off. 'Until then, it's a case of hanging on and hoping for the best.'

'Then we'd better move those pictures out of the way,' Julia said, indicating the wall.

Together they began lifting the pictures off the floor, balancing them on chairs so that they were clear of the water. Some of them were heavy, and after a while they were both breathing hard.

'Let's sit down,' he said.

As he spoke he returned to the pipe, settled beside it and began winding more tape. She went to sit on the other side.

'Are you all right?' he asked. 'It's hard work for someone who's been ill recently.'

'Yes, I'm fine. I've been feeling better ever since I kicked the door in.' She laughed. 'I think that's what I've really been needing all this time.'

'To kick a door in?' he asked, startled.

'Yes. It's one of the great healing experiences of life.' She gave a sigh of satisfaction.

'Well, it certainly seems to have done you some good,' he observed. 'You look more alive than I've ever seen you.'

'I feel it,' she said.

She was about to stretch luxuriously, but then she realised that this wasn't safe. Vincenzo was a big man and his jacket hung on her in a manner that revealed a lot, even with the darkness to help her.

And even the darkness didn't help very much. They were sitting by the window, and enough light came in to make life difficult.

'How did you come to be up here?' she asked quickly.

'I was going to ask you the same question,' he said, taking elaborate care not to look at her.

'You first.'

'I saw the door hanging from one hinge down below. I thought it must have been smashed in by a tank.'

'No, just little me,' she quipped lightly.

'I came up to see what was happening. If it's not a rude question, how do you come to be here?'

'I saw the water coming through in the room underneath. It's ruining the ceiling fresco. Honestly, the clown who owns this place ought to be shot for not looking after it properly.'

'Really,' he said with a dry irony that she missed.

'What a fool he must be,' she said indignantly, 'taking stupid risks with the water!'

'The water is cut off.'

'But nobody thought to drain that tank, did they? Or check the antiquated pipes.'

'No, you're right,' he said quietly.

'Well, there you are. He's an idiot.'

'Will you stop flailing your arms about like that?' he demanded. 'At least, if you want me to behave like a gentleman.'

'What?' She looked down at herself and grabbed the edges of the jacket together again. 'Oh, that!'

'Yes, oh, that!' He was looking away from her. 'Can I turn back?'

'Sure. No problem. There's not a lot to me, anyway,' she declared hilariously.

His mouth twisted in mocking humour. 'Shouldn't I be the judge of that?'

Her answer was to pull the edges apart again and look right down, burying her head deep in the gap.

'Nope,' she said, emerging and drawing the edges together again. 'Nothing there worth looking at. Take my word for it.'

'If you say so.'

He stared at her, startled by the change that had come into her face. Her eyes were brilliant and she seemed to be almost in a state of exaltation, tossing her long hair back from her face so that Vincenzo had one of his rare chances to see it properly.

Where had the wraith of the last week gone? he wondered. This woman had an almost demonic energy.

'Anyway, why are you getting so worked up?' he asked. 'Why do you care so much?'

'Everyone should care about great beauty,' she said firmly. 'It can't defend itself. It has to be protected and cherished. It's not just ours. It belongs to all the people who come after us.'

'But why do *you* care so much?' he persisted. 'Are you an artist?'

'I'm—' The question seemed to bring her up short, like a shot from a gun.

'That's not important,' she resumed quickly. 'The Count di Montese should be ashamed of himself, and you can tell him I said so.'

'What makes you think I know him?'

'You know him well enough to summon a plumber to his house. Of course you might be the caretaker, in which case you're doing a rotten job. Still,' she added, tossing him an olive branch, 'maybe you couldn't be expected to know about that fresco.'

'Tell me about it.'

'It's a genuine Veronese, sixteenth century. I suppose the owner would have sold it off with the rest if it wasn't painted on the ceiling.'

'Very possibly,' he murmured wryly. 'By the way, the room below this is his bedroom. What shall I say if he asks why you were there?'

'Tell him he's lucky I was.'

Vincenzo grinned. 'I will.'

'I was just looking around. Snooping, I suppose you'd say.'

He grinned. 'Yes, I expect I would. If I tell the owner he'll kick you out.'

'Then I'll kick him back,' she said. 'Don't forget my kicking foot has had some practice today. I hope he doesn't dare to try to make me pay for that door.'

'He probably will,' Vincenzo assured her, his eyes dancing. 'He's a real stinge.'

She laughed, and her hair fell over her face.

'Oh, hang it,' she said, flicking it back over her shoulder. Looking around, she noticed a length of string lying on the floor, reached for it and used it to tie her hair back.

'That's better,' he observed. 'It's nice to be able to see your face.'

'Yes, people with my sort of forehead should never wear their hair long,' she agreed.

'What's wrong with your forehead?'

'It's low,' she said, showing him. 'Most people have foreheads that are high and curve backwards, so if they grow their hair it falls down the sides of their face. But mine's so low that long hair falls forward over my face.'

He assumed a mock serious air, making a play of inspecting her. 'Yes, I see what you—'

'What is it?' she asked when he fell silent abruptly.

'Nothing—that is—I don't know.'

Once more he'd been assailed by the odd feeling he'd had the first night, that something about her was mysteriously familiar.

There were sounds coming from outside, voices from

the stairs. The next moment Piero appeared, and with him a man carrying a bag of tools.

'At last,' Vincenzo said, getting to his feet.

'Mio Dio!' Piero exclaimed, looking around him.

'Yes, it could have been a disaster but for Julia. Take her downstairs, Piero, and get her warmed up.'

Julia let herself be led away to the place where there was warmth, and fresh clothes, and hot coffee. Piero laughed heartily at her story, especially the tale of how she'd criticised 'the owner'.

'It's too bad of Vincenzo not to have told you the truth,' he said. 'He *is* the owner. His full name is *Vincenzo di Montese*.'

'What? You mean he's the count? But I thought he was one of us?' she cried, almost indignant.

'So he is. What do you think makes us as we are? Is it simply not having a roof over our heads, or is there more?'

'There's much more,' she said, thinking of the last few years when she'd had a roof over her head, and still been poorer than she was now.

'Exactly. Vincenzo has his ghosts and demons, just like us. In his case it's virtually everyone or everything he's ever loved. They betray him, they die, or they're taken from him in some other way. As a boy he worshipped his father. He hadn't seen the truth about him then.'

'What truth?'

'Sheer brute selfishness. He was a gambler who cared about nothing and nobody as long as he got his thrill at the tables, no matter how huge his losses. People say he went to pieces after his wife died, and it's true he got worse then. But it was always there.

'The old count stripped this place of its valuables, so

that now all Vincenzo owns is the shell. He lost the woman he loved. They were engaged, but the marriage fell through because her family said they didn't want to see her dowry gambled away, and who can blame them?'

'Didn't they put up a fight if they loved each other?'

'Vincenzo couldn't put up a fight. He felt that he had so little to offer that it wouldn't be fair. He's a Montese, which means he has the pride of the devil.'

'But didn't *she* fight?'

Piero shrugged. 'Not really. She may have loved him in her own way, but it wasn't a through-thick-and-thin kind of way.'

'What about him?' Julia wanted to know. 'Did he love her in a through-thick-and-thin kind of way?'

'Oh, yes. He's an all-or-nothing person. When he gives it's everything. I remember their engagement party, in this very building. Gina was incredibly beautiful and knew how to show herself off. So she climbed those stairs and posed there for everyone to admire. And he stood below, looking up at her, almost worshipping. You never saw a man so radiantly happy.

'But that same night his father left the party and went to the casino. The amount of money he lost in an hour triggered the avalanche that followed, although I suppose it would have happened anyway.

'The count took his own life soon after. Having created the mess, he dumped it all on Vincenzo and made his escape. The final selfish betrayal.'

'Dear God!' she said, shocked. 'You must have known Vincenzo well if you were at the party?'

'I was there in my capacity as Europe's greatest chef.'

'Again?' she warned. 'You're repeating yourself.'

'Ah, yes, I've been a chef before, haven't I? Well, whatever. If you could have seen the look on Vincenzo's face that night—the last time he was ever happy. He loved that woman as few women are ever loved. And when she turned from him something in him died. That part of his life is over.'

'You mean he's given up women?' Julia asked with a touch of disbelief.

'Oh, no, quite the reverse. Far too many, all meaningless. He attracts them more easily than is good for him, and forgets them the same way.'

'Maybe he's the wise one,' Julia murmured.

'That's what he says, but it's sad to see a man bury the best of himself beneath bitterness. And it's got worse these last few months since he lost his sister, Bianca, the one person left that he could talk to. They were twins and they'd always been very close.

'She and her husband died in a car crash, only a few months ago, leaving him with her two children to care for. They're all the family he has left now. Everyone and everything gets taken away from him, and now he seems to feel more at home with down-and-outs.'

They heard Vincenzo and the plumber coming down the stairs, the plumber leaving, and Vincenzo approaching. Julia was standing by the window and he went straight to her, arms wide and eager. Then she was swallowed up in a huge hug.

'Thank you, thank you!' he said fiercely. 'You'll never know what you've done for me.'

'Piero's just told me who you are,' she said, struggling to breathe. 'You've got a nerve, keeping a thing like that to yourself.'

'I'm sorry,' he said unconvincingly. 'I just couldn't resist. Besides, think how much good you did me with that frank assessment of my character. Thank you for everything, Julia—or whoever.'

It was the first time he'd openly hinted that he doubted her name, and he backed off at once, saying hastily, 'I'm taking you both to supper tonight. Be ready in an hour.'

He vanished. Julia stood there, wondering at a tinge of embarrassment that had appeared in his manner.

Her clothes were all six years old, but she was thinner now and could get into them easily. She found a blue dress that was simple enough to look elegant.

She had almost nothing in the way of make-up, a touch of pink on her lips, and no more. But it had a transforming effect.

'That's better,' Piero said when he saw her. 'Let him see how nice you can look.'

'For heaven's sake, Piero!' she said, suddenly self-conscious. 'I'm not going on a date. What about you? Are you dressing up in your Sunday best?'

'Top hat and tails,' he said at once. 'What else?'

But when Vincenzo, smartly dressed in a suit, called for them Piero was still in his coat tied up with string.

'Are we going to your own restaurant?' he asked.

'We are.'

'Are you sure you should be taking me there, dressed like this?'

'Quite sure,' Vincenzo said, with the warmest smile she had ever seen from him. 'Now let's go.'

CHAPTER FOUR

VINCENZO'S restaurant was called *Il Pappagallo*, the parrot, and stood down a street so narrow that Julia could have touched both sides at once. The lights beamed out onto the wet stones, and through the windows she could see an inviting scene.

It was a small place with perhaps a dozen tables, lit by coloured lamps. A glance at the diners showed Julia why Piero had been reluctant to come here among those well-dressed people. But Vincenzo had overruled him for friendship's sake, and she liked him for it.

He led them inside and right through the restaurant to the rear door, which he opened, revealing more tables outside.

'Normally we couldn't eat outside at this time of year,' he said, 'but it's a mild night, and I think you'll enjoy the view of the Grand Canal.'

She had partly seen it before through the *palazzo* windows, but now she saw the whole wide expanse, busy with traffic. Behind the *vaporetti* and the gondolas rose the Rialto Bridge, floodlit blue against the night sky.

'Let me take your order,' Vincenzo said. 'I think we'll start with champagne because this is a celebration.'

She'd forgotten what champagne tasted like. She'd forgotten what a celebration was.

'We serve the finest food in Venice,' Vincenzo declared, and a glance at the menu proved it.

She returned it to him. 'Order for me, please.'

52

The champagne arrived and Vincenzo poured for them all in tall, fluted glasses.

'Thank you,' he said, raising his glass to her. 'Thank you—Julia?'

'Julia,' she said, meeting his eyes, refusing to give him the satisfaction of confirming or denying her name.

Piero was looking gleefully from one to the other. She guessed he was imagining a possible romance. She shrugged the thought away, but she supposed his mistake was understandable. Many women would find Vincenzo irresistible. It wasn't a matter of looks, because strictly speaking he wasn't handsome. His nose was a little too long and irregular for that.

It was hard to tell the shape of his mouth because it changed constantly, smiling, grimacing, always reflecting his mood, which wasn't always amiable. There was a touch of pride there, and more than a touch of defensiveness.

No, it wasn't features, she decided, but something else, an indescribable mixture of charm, bitter comedy and arrogance, something unmistakably Italian. It was there in his dark, slightly sunken eyes, with their gleam that was so hard to read. A woman could drive herself distracted trying to fathom that gleam, and doubtless many women had. There was a time when she herself might have been intrigued.

But the next moment, as if to tell her to be honest with herself, she was assailed by the memory of lying beneath him on the attic floor, so that the hot, sweet sensation began to rise up in her from the pit of her stomach, threatening to overcome her completely.

She drew a long, ragged breath against the threat, refusing to give in. She was stronger than that.

Piero provided a kind of distraction, rejoicing in the champagne, pronouncing it excellent.

'Only the best,' Vincenzo said.

'Yes, it is,' she agreed, for the sake of something to say.

Vincenzo nodded. 'I thought you'd know about that.'

She pulled herself together, refusing to let him overcome her, even though he had no idea that he was doing so.

'Maybe I don't know,' she parried. 'Maybe I only said "Yes" to sound knowledgeable. Anyone can do that.'

'True. But not everyone would know about Correggio and Veronese.'

'I was guessing.'

'No, you weren't,' he said quietly.

She was getting her second wind and was able to say, 'Well, it's not your concern, and who are you to lecture me about people concealing their identity?'

'Can't you two go five minutes without bickering?' Piero asked plaintively.

'I'm not bickering,' Vincenzo said. 'She's bickering.'

'I'm not.'

'You are.'

'Stop it, the pair of you,' Piero commanded.

As one they turned on him.

'Why?' Julia asked. 'What's wrong with bickering? It's as good a way of communicating as any other.'

'That's what I always say,' Vincenzo agreed at once.

He met her eyes and she found herself reluctantly discovering that she was wrong. There *was* a better way of communicating. The look he was giving her was wicked, and it contained the kind of shared understanding she knew she would be wiser to avoid.

Piero raised his glass.

'I foresee a very interesting evening,' he said with relish.

'Can we eat the first course before we have to fight another round?' Vincenzo asked.

It was her first experience of Venetian cuisine, with its intriguing variety. A dish described simply as 'rice and peas' turned out also to contain onions, veal, butter and broth.

They drank *Prosecco* from hand-blown pink, opalescent glasses.

'They come from home,' Vincenzo said. 'There were some things I was damned if I was going to sell.'

'They're beautiful,' she said, turning a glass between her fingers. 'I can understand you wanting to keep them.'

'My father gave me the first wine I ever tasted in one of these,' he remembered. 'I was only a boy, and I felt like such a big man, sitting there with him.'

You idolised him, she thought, remembering Piero's words. *And he betrayed you.*

'Isn't it risky using them in a restaurant?' she asked.

'These aren't for the ordinary customers. I keep them for special friends. Let's drink a toast.'

They solemnly raised their glasses. Somewhere inside her she could feel a knot of tension begin to unravel. There were still good times to be had.

'Are you warm enough out here?' Vincenzo asked her. 'Would you prefer a table inside?'

'No, this is nice.'

'We have the odd fine night, even in December. It's after Christmas that it gets really bad.'

When the rice and peas had been cleared away she saw Vincenzo look up and meet the eye of a very pretty waitress, who returned a questioning smile, to which he responded with a wink and a nod of the head.

'Do you mind doing your flirting elsewhere?' Piero asked severely.

'I'm not flirting,' Vincenzo defended himself. 'I was signalling to Celia to bring in the next course.'

'And you had to do that with a wink?' Julia enquired humorously.

'I'm trying to appeal to her. She's going to vanish next week, just when I'm going to need her most.'

'But I thought you didn't need too many staff at this time of year,' Julia said.

'It's true the summer rush is over, but in the run-up to Christmas there's a mini-rush. I shed staff in October and increase them in December. In January I shed them again, then increase them in February just before the Carnival. A lot of workers like it that way—a few weeks on, a few weeks off. But Celia's going off just when I need her on. I've begged and pleaded—'

'You've winked and smiled—' Julia supplied.

'Right. And all to no avail.'

'You mean that this young female is immune to your charm?' Piero asked, shocked.

'His what?' Julia asked.

'His charm. *Chaa-aarm.* You must have heard of it?'

'Yes, but nobody told me Vincenzo was supposed to have any.'

'Very funny, the pair of you,' Vincenzo said, eyeing them both balefully.

Celia appeared at the table bearing a large terracotta pot, in which was an eel, cooked in bay leaves.

'This is a speciality of Murano, the island where the glass-blowing is centred,' Vincenzo explained. 'It was once cooked over hot coals actually in the glass furnaces. I can't compete with that. I have to use modern ovens, but I think it'll taste all right.'

When Celia had finished serving the eel he took her hand, gazing up into her eyes, pleading. His words were in Venetian but Julia got the gist of them without trouble, and even managed to decipher, 'My love, I implore you.'

Even if it was all play-acting, she thought, it had a kind of magic that a woman would do well to beware. Celia seemed in no danger. She giggled and departed.

'I guess I can't persuade Celia.' He sighed. 'Tonight's her last night. She's about to get married and go on her honeymoon. That's her fiancé over there. *Ciao*, Enrico.'

A burly man grinned at him from another table. Vincenzo grinned back in good fellowship. Julia concentrated on her food, trying not to be glad that Celia had a fiancé.

As they ate the eel, washed down with Soave, her feeling of well-being increased. She had forgotten many things about the real world: good food, fine wines, a man who had dark, intense eyes, and turned them on her, inviting her to understand their meaning.

She was too wise to accept that invitation, but the understanding was there, whether she wanted it or not. It tingled in her senses, it ached in her heart, so long starved of the joyous emotions. It told her that she must risk just this one evening.

After the eel came wild duck. While it was being served she turned to look out over the canal.

'Have you ever been to Venice before?' Vincenzo asked.

'No. I always meant to, but somehow it never happened.'

'Not even when you were studying art? Please, Julia,' he added quickly as she looked up, 'let's not pretend about that, at least. You recognised a Correggio and a

Veronese at the first glance, and you can't turn the clock back to before it happened. You're an artist.'

'An art restorer,' she conceded reluctantly. 'At one time I fancied myself as a great painter, but my only talent turned out to be for imitating other people's styles.'

'You must have studied in Italy. That's how you know the language, right?'

'I studied in Rome, and Florence,' she agreed.

'Then I'll enjoy showing you the whole house, although it's only a ghost of itself now. I wish you could have seen it in its glory days.'

'You've lost everything, haven't you?' she said gently.

'Just about.' He glanced at Piero and lowered his voice. 'Do I have any secrets left?'

'Not many.'

'Good, then I needn't bore you with the whole story. Now let's eat. With duck we drink Amarone.'

He filled their glasses with the red wine that had just been brought to the table. Julia sipped it with relish and looked back at the canal.

'I should like to see Venice in summer,' she said, 'when it's bright and cheerful, not dark and menacing as it is now.' She glanced at him, smiling. 'I'm sorry, I don't mean to be rude about your city.'

'But you're right. It's true, Venice can be menacing, especially on quiet winter nights. Its history has been one of blood as well as romance, and even today there are times when an assassin seems to lurk around each corner, and peril haunts every shadow.

'In the summer the tourists arrive and say, "How pretty! How quaint!" but if Venice were only pretty and quaint it would soon grow dull.'

'Pretty and quaint are two words that never occurred

to me,' she said wryly. 'That's what sleeping on the stones can do for you.'

His grin broadened into a laugh, and she realised how seldom there was real amusement in his face. It was there now, and it delighted her.

'You have all my sympathy,' he said. 'Nowhere else are the stones as hard as ours. Venice is the loveliest city in the world, but it can also be the most cruel. And that's why I wouldn't live anywhere else. Does that sound crazy?'

'No, I understand it. You can't study art for long without knowing that anything that's merely pretty grows tedious very soon.'

He nodded.

'In the same way, a woman who has only looks soon palls. Sadly, it takes a man time to understand that, and when he's found out it may be too late. The woman with the dark, dangerous heart may be already beyond his reach.'

She gave a wry smile.

'That's very nice talk, but aren't you deluding yourself?'

'Am I?'

'How many men truly want a woman with a dark, dangerous heart?'

'The discriminating ones, perhaps.'

'And how many men are discriminating? You don't need a dangerous heart to do the washing-up.'

'You mean that it would be an attribute of a mistress, rather than a wife?'

'I mean that you're spinning glittering fantasies in the air. They have no reality behind them.'

'I didn't realise that you knew me so well.'

The words were lightly spoken, but with a slight warning edge. In truth, she didn't know him at all.

'I like to choose my own fantasies,' he said lightly. 'And I decide what they mean.'

His eyes challenged her. She met the challenge and threw it back, but she could think of no words that weren't more perilous than silence.

She glanced at Piero, afraid that she would find him regarding them with gleeful interest, but he was engaged in a mad flirtation with Celia, who was laughing at his jokes, and giving him extra food and wine. He consumed everything with gusto, especially the wine, and it was clear that he was soon headed for blissful oblivion.

Seeing him so absorbed, she began to feel as though she were alone with Vincenzo, who didn't take his eyes from her.

'Why won't you tell me who you are?' he asked softly. 'And why you are here. I might be able to help.'

At one time she would have replied quickly that nobody could help her. Now she merely shook her head.

'You'll have to tell someone, some time. Why not me?'

'Because you get too close.'

'People who care should get too close. Don't keep yourself shut away. Why are you smiling like that?'

'Nothing,' she said. 'I wasn't really.'

'There you go again, hiding. You're like someone who barely exists. I know only what you choose to tell, and, since that's almost nothing, it's like being able to see right through you. I don't know your name or what brought you here, or why you try so hard to conceal yourself in the dark.'

'The light frightens me,' she whispered.

'But why? You answer one question and a thousand others spring up. When will your mysteries end?'

'They won't. Vincenzo, please, it's better if you don't seek to know them.'

'Better for whom?'

'For both of us, but mostly for you.'

'Then you already know what's happening to me.'

'Don't. Don't say it. Don't think it. Don't let it happen.'

'Don't you want to be loved?'

'How can I tell? What is it like?'

'Are you saying that no man has ever loved you?'

'Please—'

'No man has wanted to take you in his arms and lie with you, demanded the right to claim and possess you in every way?'

'It doesn't matter what they've wanted,' she told him. 'Who cares what men say? Only fools believe them. No, I've never been loved. I might have thought so, but we all have these little self-delusions.'

'Until the truth breaks in at last,' he agreed. 'There's nothing you can tell me about self-delusion. But the biggest self-delusion of all is to tell ourselves that we can manage without love in future.'

'Look at my face,' she said, drawing the hair back. 'I'm an old woman.'

'No, you're not. There's suffering in your face, but not age. You're a young woman who's learned to feel old inside.'

She smiled in ironic acknowledgement. 'You see too much.'

His fingers brushed her hand, and she could feel in the light touch everything he was trying to say.

'Don't,' she warned him. 'Don't reach out to me.'

'Suppose I want to?'

'But I can't reach back. Can't you understand? I have nothing to give.'

His fingers possessed hers and he didn't look at her directly as he said, 'Perhaps I don't want you to give, but to take.'

'It makes no difference,' she said sadly. 'I no longer know how to do either. I forgot both long ago.'

'How long?'

She took a deep breath. 'Six years, two months and four days.'

The stark precision of the answer startled him.

'And what happened, six years, two months and four days ago?' he asked.

'I packed my feelings away in an iron chest marked, "No longer required". Then I buried that chest too deep to be found again. I've even forgotten where it is.'

'I don't believe that. You'll remember when you want to. Can't I help you do it?'

'I don't want to remember,' she whispered. 'It hurts too much. Tell me, Vincenzo, how deep is your iron chest buried?'

'Not as deep as I'd like. I find I can't do without those feelings, even if they hurt. Better be hurt than dead inside.'

'Meaning I'm a coward?' she demanded swiftly.

'I didn't say that.'

'You implied it.'

'Why are you trying to quarrel with me?' he asked quietly.

'Perhaps because I really am a coward,' she admitted after a moment. 'I have so little courage left, and I need all of it.'

'And I threaten it?'

'Yes,' she whispered. 'Yes, you do.'

She had said that she could not reach out, but she knew how fatally easy it would be to seek warmth from this man who seemed to have so much to give. But it would deflect her from her true purpose, and nothing must be allowed to do that.

'You do,' she repeated.

'Don't be afraid of me.'

'I'm not afraid of you, *but I will not let you in*. Do you understand?'

'I told myself the same thing about you, but somehow you got in.'

'I wasn't trying to,' she said quickly.

'I know. Maybe that's how you managed it. You were there before I could put my defences in place.'

'You're forgetting that I don't really exist,' she said.

She tried to speak lightly, but it was hard, and he made it harder by coming back swiftly with, 'Sometimes I wish you didn't. You're trouble. I don't know how or why, but you're big trouble, and you're going to throw my life in turmoil.'

'Just ignore me.'

'That's a dishonest reply.' For a moment he was angry. 'You know it's too late for that.'

'Yes,' she murmured after a moment. 'Yes, it's too late. It's much too late.'

Hours had passed. Customers were leaving the restaurant, and lights were going off. Lost in her awareness of Vincenzo, Julia hardly realised it was happening.

A waiter approached them to say that Vincenzo was needed for some formality. When he'd gone Julia turned back to Piero, and found him, as she'd expected, deeply, blissfully asleep.

Vincenzo returned as the last customer was leaving, and smiled at the sight of their friend.

'He'd better stay here tonight,' he said. 'There's a little room behind the kitchen where I sometimes sleep when I'm working late.'

He summoned a waiter. Together they carried Piero through the kitchens into the tiny bedroom and laid him gently on the bed.

'You'd better stay here, too,' he told Julia. 'You can have the apartment upstairs that Celia has just vacated.'

He showed her up the narrow staircase into the tiny apartment. Celia had stripped the bed before leaving, and he helped her make it up.

'Thank you,' she said. 'But there was no need for you to take so much trouble. I could have gone back.'

'No,' he said at once. 'I don't want you sleeping in that huge, empty place alone. I couldn't feel easy about you.'

'You don't have to look after me,' she said with a little smile. Then she gave a little laugh. 'Except that you do, all the time, don't you? I just hate admitting it, which isn't very nice of me.'

Her voice fell softly on his ears and caused an ache inside him. She worked so hard to keep her gentler side hidden that when she allowed him a sudden glimpse it caught him off guard.

He came closer, looking at her with hot, dark eyes. He remembered another time when he'd looked at her like this. Then he'd held her in his arms, kissing her, and she had known nothing about it. She knew nothing now.

She had felt soft and good against his body, and her lips had been sweet against his. That sweetness had taken possession of him, making him long to kiss her more deeply, although he'd known he must not do so while she was asleep. Instead he had kissed her eyes and her tears.

But for her it hadn't happened. That thought was very bitter to him.

Unable to stop himself, he brushed her cheek with gentle fingers. She didn't draw away, only looked at him sadly, quite still.

'Vincenzo,' she said at last.

'Hush,' he begged. 'Say nothing.'

His fingers continued their way down her cheek and across the soft contours of her mouth. He was entranced, absorbed by her, lost in her. He touched her cheek and her mouth again with fingertips that barely brushed them, yet which seemed to burn her.

She tried to protest, but no words would come. She should stop him, but she lacked the will. This had been inevitable since a few hours ago, when she'd become aware of him as a man. She should have taken flight then, when there had still been time. Except that there had never been time.

He was going to kiss her, and she wanted it with an intensity that shocked her. It was against every plan she had made, but suddenly that no longer mattered. She could feel her hands tightening on him, pulling him forward until his lips touched hers.

They felt strangely familiar, as though they had kissed before in some other life. But in her other life there had been no kisses, no warmth or sweetness, or gentleness of lips teasing hers, part plea, part command, part exploration.

'Who are you?' he whispered against her lips.

'It doesn't matter,' she said through her swimming senses. 'I'm not real.'

'You're real now—in my arms.'

'Only here,' she whispered.

'The rest doesn't matter. Kiss me—kiss me.'

She did as he wanted, finding that after the years alone she still knew how to tease and incite a man. It was an intoxicating discovery and it sent her a little wild.

Now she allowed her hands and mouth to do as they pleased, and the things that pleased them were sensual, outrageous, experienced. He was right. This alone was real, and everything in her wanted to yield to it.

With every movement she made Vincenzo felt shock flowing along his nerves. He'd suspected the fires inside and it had tormented him, but now he knew for certain. He'd partly discovered the truth that afternoon when he'd discovered that her breasts were surprisingly generous, given her apparently boyish figure.

All the sensuality she normally kept banked down was flaming in his arms now, inciting him to explore her further, wanting more. He didn't know her real name, but her name no longer mattered. This woman was coming back to life, and he knew that he, and no other, must be the man to make it happen.

She kissed dreamily, but like a woman who understood a man's body, and every soft touch lured him on. Entranced, he dropped his lips to the base of her throat, moving them in soft, teasing movements and sensing her heated response. His own response was roaring out of control.

Only she could stop him now, and she made no attempt to do so. When he began to remove her clothes she trembled, but was removing his at the same time. It was she who drew him to the bed, and after that nothing could have stopped him.

CHAPTER FIVE

MY FIRST man in six years.

The thought came to Julia as the dawn crept in. The night had been hot and fervent, and it had left her feeling at ease in a way she had forgotten. The sheer sense of blinding, physical release had at first stunned, then invigorated her.

They had claimed each other again and again. After the first time it was she who had taken the initiative, voraciously demanding as she felt her body return to life. And he had responded with unflagging vigour.

Six years of cramped frustration, deprivation, ending in one night of blazing fulfilment.

Images came back to her: his body, hard, lean and strong, his love-making, a mingling of power and tenderness, with the power becoming predominant as he'd sensed her need.

My first in six years. And before that—ah, well!

Before that there had been passionate adoration given to the wrong man, who had betrayed it and left her with a smashed life to endure.

She sat up, careful not to awaken Vincenzo, who slept silently and heavily, as though exhausted. It was a tight fit in the narrow bed, especially as he stretched out in abandon.

He'd made love like that, she thought, with an abandon that had startled her, so different was it from the controlled surface he presented to the world.

She hadn't meant to take him to bed, so she told herself. Either that or she had meant it from the first moment. One of the two. Did it matter which?

Their aggressive encounter in the attic had awoken in her a physical hunger, long suppressed, and satisfying it had become urgent.

I didn't think I was like that, she thought wryly. But I suppose after so long…

He moved in his sleep and stretched out a hand, seeking until he encountered her skin. Then it stopped, lying gently against her as though nothing else in the world mattered.

Strangely, it was that gesture that alarmed her. If he'd grasped her robustly she would have cheerfully returned to the fray. But the touch against her body was tender. It spoke of emotion, and she knew that emotion must be kept out of this. Only that way could she feel safe.

After a moment she moved his hand away.

Vincenzo stirred and stretched, almost pushing her out of the tiny bed. She laughed, clinging on for dear life, and he awoke to find her looking down at him. He grinned, remembering the night they had passed together.

Her passion had astounded him. More accustomed to her mental and emotional defensiveness, he'd been taken aback by her sensual abandon. She'd given everything with fierce generosity and demanded everything with an equally fierce appetite. When he had been satiated she had been ready to start again.

Now she looked fresh, light-hearted and mysteriously younger. There was even a teasing look in her eyes that had never been there before.

'That was fun,' she said.

The words brought him back down to earth. 'Fun' described a race through the canals, a brilliant costume for

Carnival. It bore no relation to the experience that had just shaken him to his roots.

But he answered her in kind, speaking lightly.

'I'm glad you feel the night wasn't wasted.'

She was silent, but shook her head, teasing.

He reached out so that she could take his hand, then he would draw her closer for a kiss. But instead she laughed and got to her feet, looking around for something to throw over her nakedness. Finding his shirt on the floor, she seized that.

'Spoilsport,' he sighed.

She chuckled and left the room, heading for the kitchen. He followed at once, catching up, putting his arms about her from behind, and nuzzling her hair.

'All right?' he asked softly.

'Of course,' she said brightly. 'Everything's fine.'

He partly withdrew his hands, just as far as her shoulders. 'That's good,' he said quietly.

'Do you know how I make coffee in this kitchen?' she asked with a laugh.

'I'll make it.'

'Lovely. Then we'll go down and see if Piero's awake yet. He and I should be going soon.'

He dropped his hands.

'Whatever you say.'

She turned suddenly. 'There's something you should know. Don't expect too much from me just now. I'm not used to being in the land of the living. I've forgotten how things are done there.'

He frowned, alerted by a new note in her voice, but not understanding it. 'The land of the living? I don't understand.'

'For the last six years I've been in prison.'

*   *   *

Julia had told Vincenzo that kicking the door in had been one of the great healing experiences of life, and it was true. With that one blow she had put her lethargy behind her, and was ready for the task that had brought her here.

Walking home with Piero that morning, she bought a map, and studied it as soon as they were inside.

'Can I help?' he asked.

'I want to go to the island of Murano.'

'Take the waterbus. It's about a twenty-minute journey. I'll show you the exact place. Are you going to look at some of the glass-blowing factories?'

'No, I'm looking for a man. His name is Bruce Haydon. He has relatives there and they'll know where he is now.'

'Is he Italian?'

'No, he's English. He had some Italian family on his mother's side, but he's lived mostly in England.'

She knew he was hoping to hear more, and she was foolish to keep silent. She should simply say that Bruce Haydon had once been her husband; that he had betrayed her vilely and condemned her to hell. But just now she wasn't ready to say the words.

When she'd changed back into her jeans he led her to the San Zaccaria landing stage, and waited with her while the boat arrived. Passengers poured off, more passengers poured on. As she was about to turn away Piero tightened his grip on her arm.

'Come back safely,' he said.

'Yes, I will,' she promised him in a gentle voice.

As the boat drew away from the landing stage she looked back and saw Piero standing where she had left him. He remained motionless, growing smaller until she could no longer see him.

At last the boat reached the landing stage at Murano.

It was a small island, constructed, like Venice, of canals and bridges, famous for its glass-blowing, but without the glamour of the main city.

With the aid of the map she was able to discover a row of houses beside a canal, and began to make her way along, searching for one front door.

Then it was there before her, the front door with a brass plaque proclaiming that here lived Signor and Signora Montressi, the name of Bruce's Italian relatives. Luck was with her.

She rang the bell and waited. But there was no reply.

She told herself she must be patient.

She found a café and ordered coffee and sandwiches. From her bag, she took a small photo album in which she kept pictures to show people who might have seen him. It wasn't very up to date. None of the photographs was less than six years old.

The first one was a wedding picture, showing a handsome man, grinning with delight. There was no sign of his bride. Julia had cut her out of the picture.

He had dark hair and eyes, but, although his Italian ancestry was visible, his face was slightly too fleshy for the kind of dramatic looks that Vincenzo had. He lacked Vincenzo's intensity too, parading instead an air of self-satisfaction.

She stopped and gave an exclamation of annoyance at herself. Forget Vincenzo! Comparing every other man with him was futile. For many reasons.

But there was no way to forget Vincenzo. Picro had said, 'He's an all or nothing person. When he gives it's everything.'

After last night she knew that it was true.

But Piero had also said Vincenzo had too many women, 'all meaningless'.

So he was like herself, she thought. Nature had shaped him one way, and hard lessons had shaped him differently.

In that hot, dark night he'd become his true self again, giving generously, endlessly, revealing himself to her with no defences, nothing held back.

And it shamed her that she'd only half responded, revelling in the physical pleasure that he gave so expertly, returning it with every skill at her command, but giving nothing else. Her heart was still safely hoarded in her own control.

She remembered the scene in the kitchen that morning. He'd been tender and affectionate, seeking to evoke the same in her. She'd disappointed him because she was unable to do anything else.

Blurting out that she'd been in prison had been an impulse, instantly regretted. After that she hadn't been able to get away from him fast enough, and he'd sensed it, and let her go, saying little.

She returned to the pictures, trying to concentrate on them and forget Vincenzo.

After the wedding snap came a selection of photographs taken over the next four years, during which the man put on a little weight, but continued to be good-looking and pleased with himself.

'Whatever did I see in you?' she asked the grinning head. 'Well, I paid a heavy price for it.'

He filled the first half of the book. In the second half there was a different set of pictures.

They showed a baby, starting with the day it was born. Then the child became gradually larger and prettier, with curly blonde hair and shining eyes. And always she was laughing.

Julia slammed the album shut, closing her eyes and

73

fighting back the tears. For a moment she sat there, rigid, aching, while heartbreak tore her apart.

At last the storm passed, and she forced herself to return to reality and behave normally.

'Not much longer,' she promised herself. 'Not much longer.'

The weak moment was behind her.

Her second visit to the house was equally fruitless. It was dark before she returned a third time.

As she turned into the canal-side street she could see the lights in the windows. The door was opened by a pretty young girl.

'Signora Montressi?' Julia asked.

'Oh, no, she and her husband have gone until after Christmas. They're taking a Caribbean cruise. They left three days ago. I'm afraid that's all I know. I only come in to feed the cat. They'll be back in January.'

She almost ran away, needing to be alone to absorb the shock. To have got so close and then have the prize snatched out of reach.

She walked about aimlessly for a long time before catching the boat back across the lagoon. It was late but there were still plenty of travellers, and she stood looking over the rail at the black water. It would be a relief to get home.

Home. How strange that she should think of the *palazzo* as home. Yet there would be a warm welcome for her there, and what else was home but that?

'Scusi—scusi—'

She moved as someone squeezed past her. At the same moment the boat ploughed into an extra high wave, causing it to lurch. As she grabbed the rail the strap of her bag began to slide down her arm. She twisted, trying to save it, and lost her grip.

As she watched the bag went sailing down into the water, carrying with it her precious album of pictures.

Vincenzo would have liked to get out of the dinner party at the Danieli Hotel, but he had promised and must keep his word. So he did his duty, sat next to an heiress who'd plainly heard of his circumstances, smiled, behaved with charm, concealed his boredom, and forgot her the moment the party was over.

From the hotel it was a short walk home, past San Zaccaria, and across St Mark's. Preoccupied with his thoughts, he'd actually walked past the landing stage before he realised what he'd seen. He turned sharply back.

'Piero,' he said. 'What are you doing here?'

'Waiting for her boat,' the old man said.

Vincenzo's heart sank. It was usually in the afternoons that Piero came here on his fruitless mission. If he'd started coming so late at night, he must be getting worse.

'I don't think there are any more boats tonight,' he said, laying his hand on Piero's shoulder.

'There's one more,' Piero said calmly. 'She'll be on that.'

'Piero, please—' It tore him apart to see the frail old man standing in the cold wind, clinging onto futile hope.

'There it is,' Piero said suddenly.

In the distance they could see lights moving towards them. Sick at heart, Vincenzo watched as it made its slow journey.

'She went to Murano,' Piero said. 'I put her on the boat here this morning.'

'Her? You mean Julia?'

'Of course. Who did you think I meant?'

'Well—I was a bit confused. I probably had too much to drink. What's this about Murano?'

'She went there looking for someone called Bruce Haydon.'

After a moment they both saw her standing by the rail. As the boat drew nearer she seemed to notice them suddenly. A smile broke over her face and she waved.

The two men waved back, and Vincenzo saw that Piero's face wore a look of total happiness. He wondered who the old man was seeing on the approaching boat.

At last it reached the landing stage and passengers came streaming off. Piero went forward, his arms outstretched, and Julia hugged him eagerly.

'You're back,' he said. 'You came home.'

'Home,' she said. 'Yes, that's what I was thinking.'

'Thank goodness you got back safely,' Vincenzo said. 'We were a bit concerned.'

She seemed to see him for the first time.

'There was no need,' she replied. 'I wasn't lost.'

'We didn't know that. Well, it doesn't matter. You're safe now.'

The three of them began to walk back across St Mark's Piazza and into the labyrinth of canals and little alleys that led home. Vincenzo kept firm hold of her arm, until she firmly disengaged herself.

She was angry with him again for knowing her secret—that she'd been in prison—even though she herself had disclosed it. And she was angry with herself for doing so.

'I'm all right,' she said. 'I don't need help.'

'Yes, you do. Even prickly, awkward you. And don't walk away from me when I'm trying to talk to you.'

'Don't talk to me when I'm trying to walk away.'

'If you aren't the most—'

'It's no use trying to reason with her,' Piero said. 'I've

tried, but it's pointless.' He added in a deliberately pro-
vocative tone, 'After all, she's a woman.'

Julia turned and walked backwards, her eyes fixed
on him.

'I'd stamp on your feet if I had the energy,' she teased.

Piero's answer to this was a little dance. 'You couldn't
do it,' he asserted. 'I used to dance leading roles with the
Royal Ballet in London.'

She began to imitate him, and they hopped back and
forth while passers-by gave them a wide berth, and
Vincenzo watched them, grinning.

Later, as the three of them sat by the stove Vincenzo
said, 'Did things go well?'

'No,' she said robustly, 'things went just about as
badly as they could. The people I went to see are on a
cruise. I missed them by three days, and they won't be
back until January. I had an album of pictures of the man
I'm seeking, and on the way home it fell overboard. So
now I don't even have that.'

Vincenzo frowned. 'For someone who's just lost everything you're astonishingly cheerful.'

'I'm not cheerful, just mad. Mad-angry, not mad-crazy.
I've been acting like a wimp, but now I'm done with
weakness. When the pictures went overboard I was dev-
astated for a whole minute, but then something inside me
said, "That's it! Time to fight back."'

'The man you're looking for,' Vincenzo said carefully,
'is he anything to do with—what you told me last night?'

'Anything to do with my being in prison? Yes, he put
me there. He cheated and lied and managed to get me
locked up for his crime.' She surveyed them both. 'He's
my husband.'

Piero turned his head slowly. Vincenzo stirred.

'My name isn't Julia. It's Sophie Haydon. My husband

was Bruce Haydon. My mother warned me against him, but I wouldn't listen. We were always a little uneasy with each other after that.'

'What about your father?' Piero asked.

'I barely knew him. He died when I was a baby. Bruce and I were married over nine years ago. We had a daughter the next year, a gorgeous little girl called Natalie. I loved her to bits. She—she's almost nine now.'

Her voice shook on the words, and she hurried on as though to prevent the others noticing.

'Bruce had a little business, import, export. It wasn't doing well and he hated it that I earned more than him. I was working as an art restorer, getting plenty of clients, starting to be employed by museums and great houses.'

'And then there was a spate of art thefts, all from houses where I'd been working. Of course the police suspected me. I knew all about the keys and burglar alarms.'

She fell silent again, staring into space for a long time. Then she jumped to her feet and began to pace up and down, her feet making a hollow, desolate sound on the tiles.

'Go on,' Vincenzo said in a strained voice.

'I was charged and put on trial.' She gave a harsh laugh. 'Bruce made me a wonderful speech about fighting it together. And I believed him. We loved each other, you see.' She gave a brief, mirthless laugh. 'That's really funny.'

She fell silent. Neither of the other two moved or spoke, respecting her grief.

'In the last few days before the trial,' she went on at last, 'my mind seemed to be working on two levels at once. On one, I just couldn't believe that they could find me guilty. On the other, I knew exactly what was going to happen. I knew they were going to take me away from

Bruce and Natalie, and I spent every moment I could with them. Bruce and I—'

She stopped. It was better not to remember those passionate nights, his declarations of undying love, lest she go mad.

'We took Natalie on a picnic. On the way back we stopped in a toy shop and she fell in love with a rabbit. So I bought it for her and she hugged it all the way home. When the trial began I'd say goodbye to her in the morning and she'd clutch that rabbit for comfort. When I came home she'd still be clutching him. The neighbour who was looking after her said she never let go of him all day.

'On the last day of the trial I got ready to leave home and Natalie began to cry. She'd never done that before, but this time it was as though she knew I wasn't coming back. She clung to me with her arms tight about my neck, crying "No, Mummy. Mummy, don't go, please don't go—please, Mummy—"'

She was shuddering, forcing herself to speak through the tears that coursed down her cheeks.

'In the end they had to force her arms away from around my neck, while she screamed and screamed. Then she curled up on the sofa, clutching her rabbit and sobbing into his fur. That was the last time I ever saw her. All she knew was that I went away and never came back. Wherever she is now, whatever she's doing, that's her last memory of me.'

She swung around suddenly and slammed her hand down on the back of a chair, clinging onto it and choking in her agony. Vincenzo rose quickly and went to her, but she straightened up before he could touch her.

'I'm all right. Where was I?'

'The trial,' he said gently.

'Oh, yes. They found me guilty. Bruce came to see me in prison a couple of times. He kept promising to bring Natalie "next time", but he never did. And then one day he didn't come. My mother told me he'd vanished, taking our little girl.

'I don't remember the next few days clearly. I know I became hysterical, and for a while I was on suicide watch. That was six years ago, and I haven't seen either of them since.

'It was him, you see. He'd copied my keys, picked my brains. He'd drive me to work and ask me to show him around, "Because I'm so interested, darling." So he knew what to look for, how to get in, how to turn off the alarm. Sometimes there were security staff, but they trusted him because he was with me. And everything he learned he sold to a gang of art thieves.

'All the thefts happened over the same weekend, then they vanished abroad, leaving me to take the blame like a tethered goat. By the time I realised how Bruce was involved he'd vanished too.'

'But surely you told the police?' Piero asked.

'Of course, but even I could hear how hollow it sounded—clutching at straws to clear myself. My sentence was longer because I'd been "unco-operative". I couldn't tell them anything, because I didn't know.

'And all the time I knew he had my little girl somewhere. I didn't know where and I couldn't find out. She was two and a half when I last saw her. Where has she been all that time? What has she been told about me? Does she have nightmares about our last moments, as I do?'

Her voice faded into a despairing whisper. After a moment she began speaking again.

'Then a couple of the pictures turned up at an auction

house. The police managed to trace the trail right back to the mastermind, and he told them everything. He hadn't long to live and he wanted to "clear his conscience", as he put it. He said Bruce used to laugh about how I trusted him, and how easy I was to delude.'

'*Bastardo!*' Vincenzo said with soft venom.

'Yes,' she agreed, 'but I suppose I should be glad of it, because that story was what cleared me. It meant that Bruce and I hadn't colluded. My conviction was quashed and I was released.'

She paced a little more before stopping by the window.

'My lawyer's fighting for compensation, but my only use for money is to pay for a proper search for Bruce, if I haven't found him by then.'

'Aren't the police looking for him?' Vincenzo suggested.

'Not as hard as I am. To them he's just another wanted man. To me he's an enemy.'

'Yes, I see,' Vincenzo said, almost to himself.

Her voice mounted in urgency.

'He wrecked my life, left me to rot in prison and took my child. I want my daughter back, *and I don't care what else happens.*'

'Have you no family to help you?' Piero asked.

'My mother died of a broken heart while I was in prison. She left me a very little money, just enough to come here and start searching for Bruce.'

'So you came to Venice to find his relatives?' Piero asked.

'Yes. They're only distant, but they might know something that could help me. I had some good friends who visited me in prison, and they used to bring stories about how Bruce had been "seen". Some of them were wildly unlikely. He was in Arizona, in China, in Australia. But

two people said they'd spotted him in Italy, once in
Rome, and more recently in Venice, crossing the Rialto
Bridge.

'That's why I went straight to the Rialto that first night.
Don't ask me what I thought I was going to do then,
because I couldn't tell you. The inside of my head was
a nightmare. Luckily the Rialto is near this place and
Piero found me on his way home. If my friend really did
see Bruce it may mean nothing, or he may be living only
a few minutes away. You might even have seen him.'

'It would help if you had some pictures of him,'
Vincenzo observed.

'I know, but my pictures went to the bottom of the
lagoon an hour ago.' She clutched her head. 'If only I'd
shown them to you last week—'

'You were full of fever last week,' Piero said. 'You
didn't know whether you were coming or going. It's just
bad luck, but we probably wouldn't have recognised him
anyway.'

She nodded. 'The Montressis are my best lead. They'll
be back in January, and then I'll hunt him down and get
my daughter back.'

'But will it be that simple?' Vincenzo asked. 'After six
years she may want to stay where she is.'

She gave him a look that chilled his blood.

'I am her mother,' she said with slow, harsh emphasis.
'She belongs with me. If anyone tries to stop me, I'll—'
She was breathing hard.

'Yes?' he asked uneasily.

She met his eyes. 'I'll do what I have to—whatever
that might be—I don't know.'

But she did know. He could see it in her face and feel
it in her determination to reveal no more. She wouldn't

put her thoughts into words because they were too terrible to be spoken.

He didn't recognise this woman. She'd freely claimed to be 'as mad as a hatter', and there were times in her delirium and sleepwalking when she'd seemed to be treading some fine line between reality and delusion. But now he saw only grim purpose in her eyes, and he wondered which side of the line she had stepped.

And who could blame her, he wondered, if her tragedy had driven her to the wrong side?

CHAPTER SIX

'So,' Vincenzo said gently, 'when you find Bruce—'

'He's going to give her back to me. If he's reasonable I'll promise him twenty-four hours' start before I point the police in his direction.'

'But then he'll get away,' Piero pointed out.

Julia turned on him.

'You don't think I'm going to keep my word, do you?' she asked scornfully. 'As soon as I'm clear with Natalie I'll put them straight onto him. After what he did to me, I'll have no remorse about anything I do to him.

'I've had plenty of time to learn to be strong. I'm a different person now. Sophie was a fool. She thought feelings were wonderful because they made her happy.'

'She doesn't sound like a fool to me,' Vincenzo said quietly.

'Oh, she was worse than that,' Julia said with an edge of contempt for her old self. 'She needed people and she believed in them. She hadn't learned that that's the quickest way to hell. But Sophie's dead and good riddance to her. Julia knows it's better to use people than trust them. She's grown wise.'

'Too wise to love?' Vincenzo asked. 'Too wise to need?'

'Too wise to feel. The one thing she learned in prison was not to feel anything.'

'Not even for her child?'

She took a sharp breath. 'That's different. She's part

of me, flesh of my flesh. It's as though someone had torn my heart out and wouldn't give it back.'

'So that's why you said you had nothing to give,' he reminded her in a low voice.

'Yes, and it was true, so believe it.'

There was a flash of anger in his eyes. 'And suppose I choose not to believe it?'

'That's your risk, but remember that I warned you.'

He was silent for a moment. Then he nodded.

'I'll be going now. Walk a little way with me.'

She followed him quietly, and as they neared the outer door he said, 'It's a long time between now and mid-January. How are you going to spend that time?'

'Sharpening my sword,' she said with grim humour.

'Don't talk like that,' he said harshly.

'Why? Because you've got some fairy-tale picture of me as sweetness and light? Maybe I was, then. Not now. Now I'm a monster who knows how to fight dirty. And I'll do it.'

He raised an eyebrow, dampening her agitation.

'I was only going to suggest a better way to pass the time. Come and work for me while Celia's away. Of course, for an artist, waitressing may seem like a comedown—'

'But for a gaolbird it's a step up,' she said lightly.

He refused to rise to the bait. 'Will you take the job?'

She hesitated. She had promised herself to beware of him. She made that promise often, and broke it constantly because he touched her heart, deny it as she might.

As if he could read her mind, Vincenzo said quietly, 'Never fear. I won't trouble you. In fact I ought to apologise.'

'For what?'

'Pressuring you. I guessed that something painful had happened, but I had no idea of anything like this.'

She smiled in mockery of herself. 'Now you know how I turned into an avenging witch. Not a pretty sight, am I?'

'I'm not judging you. What right do I have? But I can't believe that Sophie is dead. I think she's still there somewhere.'

'More fool you,' she sighed. 'You've been warned.'

'Let's leave that for the moment. You need peace and space, and I'll let you have them while you're working for me.'

'All right, I'll take the job.'

'Good. You can have the apartment over the restaurant.'

She shook her head.

'Thank you, but I'll stay here. I can't leave Piero alone now. I know he was alone before, but something's changed. I have a feeling that he needs me.'

'I thought you had no feelings.'

'This is family obligation.'

'And you two are family?'

'Not by blood, but in other ways.' She added quickly, 'And that's not an emotion either. It's survival.'

'And what about me? Am I part of the family?'

She didn't answer, and he knew he was excluded from the charmed circle.

It ought not to matter. He still had relatives with whom he would spend Christmas, leaving these two misfits to whatever comfort they could find with each other. And yet it hurt.

As the month moved towards Christmas, winking lights glinted everywhere, in shop windows, strung across the streets and over the bridges.

People called out of windows and across bridges, wishing each other, *'Buon Natale.'* Merry Christmas. Decorated trees appeared in the squares, and red-robed figures strode about the little city, waving cheerily and talking to children.

'Father Christmas,' Julia exclaimed, pleased.

'Babbo Natale,' Piero corrected her. 'That's what we call him. *Babbo* means "Father".'

'I thought that was *padre*?'

'Padre means "father" too,' Piero agreed. 'But it's more formal. *Babbo* is a kind of affectionate diminutive. Some children use it to their fathers, especially when they're very young.'

'Did Elena do that?' she asked.

'Oh, yes. I've always been *Babbo* to her, except for— well, there was a time when we argued a lot, and she started calling me *Papà*. But that's all over now, and when she comes back I'll be *Babbo* again. Hey, look over there! A whole collection of them!'

He pointed to the Grand Canal, where six red-garbed figures were rowing one gondola, accompanied by blaring Christmas music, and the subject of Elena was allowed to drop.

The week before Christmas she awoke to find Venice under snow. Delighted, she and Piero went out and walked arm in arm through the city that had been totally transformed. Snow-covered gondolas bobbed in the water, snow-covered bridges glittered over tiny canals. A brilliant, freezing sun poured down blindingly on the white blanket, and she had to shield her eyes from the glare.

Now there were musicians wandering the alleys and the *piazzas*, wearing the traditional shepherds' garb of

buckskins and woollen cloaks, and playing bagpipes. The
sweet, reedy sound pursued them to St Mark's, where
they threw snowballs, ducking and diving, laughing at
each other like people who hadn't a care in the world.

Vincenzo had insisted on giving her a generous
amount of money for saving his home from damage.
'Your caretaker's bonus,' he called it.

Julia had immediately passed it on to Piero. When he'd
demurred she'd told him that this was only half the
amount, and she was merely sharing with him. From his
sceptical look she'd doubted that he'd been fooled, but
he'd accepted the money.

'Get something warm to wear,' she told him.

But as the days went on there was no sign of new
clothes. Evidently he had other priorities, which he was
not prepared to discuss.

She was a huge success at *Il Pappagallo*. Venice was
filling up with Christmas tourists, and the restaurant was
crowded every night. Some of the customers insisted on
being served only by her.

She enjoyed this admiration, which made her laugh.
Vincenzo, she was secretly pleased to note, didn't find it
funny.

'You shouldn't let Antonnio monopolise you,' he said
as they were walking through the dark *calles* one night.
'There are plenty of other customers.'

'He's the kind who always makes sure he's noticed,'
Julia said lightly. Antonnio's persistent gallantry had
done her ego a world of good.

'And you always make sure you serve him first,'
Vincenzo growled.

'Only because he grabs that table near the kitchen.'

'Yes, so that he can grab your hand as you go past,

and devour it,' he said, as close to ill tempered as she'd ever seen him. 'In future, I'll serve him.'

She chuckled. 'He'll love that.'

'*You're* loving it.'

'Well, he did promise me a very special tip,' she mused.

'Be careful. Antonnio's "special tips" are legendary and they don't involve money.'

She took his arm. 'Oh, stop being so pompous. I'm just doing my job. And after six years shut up with women maybe I don't mind a little admiration.'

'A little admiration,' he scoffed. 'Another moment he'd have had you down on the floor.'

She didn't answer that with words, only with an ironic glance.

'I see,' he said grimly. 'Perhaps the woman who boasts of no feelings likes making me jealous?'

'The woman with no feelings says she doesn't belong to you, and you have no right to be jealous. What happened to your promise to back off and give me space?'

'I wouldn't be the first man to make a promise he can't keep.'

'Vincenzo, what are you hoping for?'

He shrugged. 'Maybe I'm waiting to meet Sophie.'

'She's gone. She died some time during my second year in gaol. She won't come back.'

'You're wrong. She never completely went away. That's why I can't free myself of you.'

They had come to a halt under a lamp that showed them to each other in bleached, unearthly hues. Her face, once too thin, had filled out a little, he realised, and lost some of its tormented look. She had fine, beautiful bone structure, and the slight extra flesh suited her, reclaiming some of her youth.

Tonight she had revelled, siren-like, in her customers' adulation, making him wonder at the different moods that turned her into so many people. Any of them, or none of them, could be the real woman, and all of them were driving him mad.

'You should try harder to free yourself from me,' she said. 'It's just a question of being strong-minded.'

'Maybe I don't want to be strong-minded.'

Snow began to fall, just a few flakes at first, then more and more. Through them she searched his face in the cold light. 'In the end I'll go away and leave you,' she whispered. 'Like everyone else.'

'I know,' he said sadly. 'But who knows when the end will be? Not tonight.'

As he spoke he gathered her into his arms, and she went into them easily, offering her lips to his kiss and returning it with passion.

She knew that very passion was her enemy. It threatened to distract her from her purpose, but she couldn't help it. He brought her back to life, and the feeling was sweet, wild, and frightening.

'No—no—' she whispered, more to herself than him.

He drew back to look at her with troubled eyes. 'Do you want me to stop?'

'No,' she said explosively, fastening her mouth on his.

She was kissing him with frantic desire, possessed by feelings that were almost too sweet to be borne. It was she who explored his mouth, almost attacking him in her urgency, teasing his lips, his tongue, feeling the deep satisfaction of his response.

'Stay with me tonight,' he murmured against her mouth.

But she shook her head. 'Not now—not tonight—'

'*Mio Dio!* How much do you think one man can stand?

You're not being fair. *He* ill-used you and you revenge yourself on us all.'

'No, it's not that, I swear it. But I don't feel that I belong anywhere. The past is over and I can't tell about the future.'

'Your daughter is all that matters to you, I know that.' He sighed, resting his forehead against hers. 'But I can be patient and hope for my turn.'

'Even if it never comes?'

'Do you believe that one day you'll get your heart's desire?'

'I have to,' she whispered.

'So do I. Let's leave it there, and hope for better times.'

He slipped his arm about her shoulders, and she leaned contentedly against him as they walked the rest of the way in the falling snow.

At midday on Christmas Eve a cannon was fired from the turrets of the Castel Sant'Angelo in Rome, and Christmas had officially begun.

She and Piero listened to it together on a battery-powered radio she'd bought. The restaurant had closed, Vincenzo had gone off to his family, and she had settled in for Christmas at the *palazzo*.

They had stocked up with seasonal goodies, including *panettone*, the traditional rich fruit cake.

'We're supposed to fast for twenty-four hours after the cannon,' Piero explained, 'but I don't believe in slavishly adhering to every tradition.'

'Neither do I,' she said. 'Let's have some cake.'

As they munched she said, 'I remember when I was a child, hanging my stocking up on Christmas Eve.'

'Children don't do that in Italy,' he explained. 'Stockings don't go up until Epiphany, January sixth.'

'I'm not waiting until then to give you your present.'

'You gave me those gloves, and the scarf, two weeks ago,' he reminded her.

'Well, I had to give them to you early before you froze to death. What happened to all that money you were supposed to be spending on yourself?'

'I gambled it away. I used to be notorious for breaking the bank at Monte Carlo.'

'All right, don't tell me. Anyway, here's some boots and warm socks. I had to guess the size.'

The size was perfect. He put them on and paraded splendidly before her. She smiled and applauded, feeling content.

'And this is yours,' he said, pulling out a small object, carefully wrapped in newspaper.

Opening it she found a china Pierrot figure in a black mask and a costume decorated with many colours. Now she knew what had become of his money. She had seen this in a shop and it cost a fortune.

'Pierrot,' she said.

'So that you don't forget me,' he said.

'Do you think I ever could? *Buon Natale*, Pierrot.'

'*Buon Natale.*'

Vincenzo's gift to her was a cell phone. He called her halfway through Christmas Day.

'It's a sad Christmas for you,' he said.

'Not really. I have my friends now, and I have hope. Is that your niece I can hear?' Behind him she could make out a little girl's laughter.

'Yes, that's Rosa.'

'It's a lovely sound,' she said wistfully.

'Your time will come. Cling onto that hope.'

'I will. *Buon Natale.*'

'*Buon Natale*—Sophie.'

She smiled and hung up without answering.

After the lull of Christmas there was an immediate flurry of business. As they were clearing up on the second night she said, 'Do you mind if I hurry away? I want to get back to Piero.'

'Isn't he all right?' Vincenzo asked quickly.

'He's got a bit of a cold. I'd just like to make a fuss of him.'

'I suppose he caught cold going to San Zaccaria.' Vincenzo groaned. 'I wish he wouldn't do that in this weather.'

'But he doesn't any more. He hasn't been there since—' She fell silent as the truth dawned on her. 'Since that day I went to Murano.'

'And we met your boat,' Vincenzo said. 'And you came ashore and hugged him.'

As Julia reached home she looked up, wondering if Piero would be there, looking out for her as he sometimes did. But there was no face at the window, and for some reason that made her start to run.

He was probably just asleep, but still—

When she entered their room she couldn't see him at first. He was lying stretched out, breathing heavily. She moved quietly, not to awaken him, but then she realised that he was unlikely to have awoken, whatever she did.

His forehead was hot to the touch, and there was an ugly rasping sound to the breath, which seemed to tear his throat.

'Piero,' she said, giving him a little shake. 'Piero!'

He opened his eyes, but only a little way.

'*Ciao, cara,*' he croaked.

'Oh, my God,' she breathed. 'This is bad. Listen, I'm going to get help for you.'

'No need,' he gasped, and his feverish hand sought hers. 'Stay here,' he whispered. 'Stay with you—only you.'

'No,' she said fiercely. 'You've got to get well. I'm calling Vincenzo. He'll know what to do.' Then, before she could choke back the idiotic words she heard herself say, 'Don't go away.'

The ghost of hilarity flickered over his gaunt features. 'I won't.'

She found her cell phone and left the room. She didn't want him to hear her call. To her relief Vincenzo answered at once.

'It's Piero,' she said. 'He's very ill. I think it could be pneumonia.'

He made a sharp sound. 'All right, stay with him. I'll call an ambulance and be right there.'

She returned to find Piero sitting up, looking around him anxiously. As soon as he saw her he stretched out an arm.

'I wanted you—you weren't there...'

He held onto her like a child, his eyes fixed on her face.

'I called Vincenzo. He's sending for an ambulance.'

'Don't want—hospital—' came the painful rasping. 'Just you. Hold onto me.'

She settled him back on the sofa, and knelt beside him, one of his hot hands in hers. He kept his eyes on her, as though seeing her was all he asked. Her heart was heavy, for something told her that the end was very near.

He knew it too, she was sure, and wanted to spend his last few moments alone with her.

She heard a noise outside and went quickly to look out

of the window. Down below, in the little garden that fronted onto the Grand Canal, she could see Vincenzo, opening the wrought-iron gate, and propping it so that it stayed open.

She returned to Piero, clasping him in her arms, and after a moment Vincenzo joined them.

'The ambulance is on its way,' he said.

As he got a better look at the old man his eyes signalled his shock, and he leaned over the back of the sofa, grasping Piero's arm warmly.

'Old friend, don't give us a fright like this.'

Piero managed a faint smile.

'Don't need—ambulance,' he croaked. He looked at Julia. 'I have—all I want—since she came back to me.'

Vincenzo frowned. Her eyes met his, reminding him of what they had realised earlier.

'He doesn't mean me,' she said softly.

Vincenzo nodded. He had understood.

'Of course I came back,' she said to Piero. 'You always knew I would, didn't you—*Babbo*?'

She hesitated only a moment before using the pet name that only his daughter had used. It was a risk, but worth it. She knew she'd guessed right when he turned a radiant face on her.

'Oh, yes,' he whispered. 'Always. I kept going to wait for you. People told me you were dead, but I knew—one day—you'd be on the boat.' A faint smile touched his lips. 'And you were.'

He gave a sigh and his eyes closed. Vincenzo's gaze met Julia's and she could see that he felt helpless.

Piero's eyes opened again and when he spoke his voice was faint.

'I was afraid—but when you saw me—you smiled— and I knew that I was forgiven.'

She drew in her breath. Suddenly her eyes were blinded with tears.

'There was nothing to forgive, *Babbo*,' she murmured.

'But there was—' he insisted weakly '—said such terrible things—you know my temper—always sorry afterwards but—this time—this time—'

His breathing came faster, more laboured. A frantic note crept into his voice. 'I didn't mean it, I didn't mean it—'

'Of course you didn't. I always knew that. I forgave you long ago.'

A smile broke over his face, and although the light was fading from him it was the most brilliant smile she had ever seen. Shining through it was the glow of happiness and peace.

Suddenly he seemed to become afraid. 'Elena—Elena—'

'I'm here—always. I love you, *Babbo*.'

'I love you, daughter.'

Vincenzo turned away, covering his eyes.

A few moments later there was the sound of footsteps outside, and a voice calling, 'Is anybody there?'

Hastily controlling himself, Vincenzo went out into the hall where two young men had arrived with the ambulance. He beckoned and they quickly followed him.

One of them gasped when he saw the room. 'What a way to have to live!' he said. 'The sooner we get him to hospital, the better.'

Julia spoke in a muffled voice. 'You're too late.'

They drew near to where the two figures clasped each other. Piero's eyes were closed and his rasping breathing had stopped. He lay quiet and peaceful.

'Poor old fellow,' said one of the young men sympathetically.

Julia laid her cheek tenderly against Piero's white hair.

'Don't feel sorry for him,' she said softly. 'He died as he wanted to, in his daughter's arms.'

The two young men took over, laying Piero gently on a trolley. Julia planted a last kiss on his forehead before he was wheeled away, down into the garden and into the ambulance boat tied up in the water.

Together they stood at the window as the ambulance pulled away down the Grand Canal, until its lights were no longer visible. When it had gone Vincenzo opened his arms and she went into them.

'I'm going to miss him so much,' she said.

'So am I. But you were right. He was happy at the end and that's what matters.' He took her face in his hands and looked down at her.

'You were wonderful,' he said tenderly.

He brushed the hair back from her face, then drew her against him, with her head on his shoulder, and they stood like that in silence for a long time.

'I'm taking you away with me,' he said at last. 'You can't live here alone.'

'All right, I'll move. But not now.' She turned back into the room, suddenly so lonely. 'I want to spend one more night here.'

Piero's few pathetic possessions were still there, including the gifts she'd given him. She sat down on the bed, lifting his gloves, looking at them, stroking them.

'Who was he really?' she asked.

'Professor Alessandro Calfani, a philosopher. Once I thought I knew him well, but now I think I never knew him in any way that mattered. Did you understand what he meant about Elena forgiving him?'

'He told me she used to call him *Babbo*, but stopped

after some kind of estrangement. It sounded as though they had a big row. I guess when he wanted to say sorry, it was too late.'

'But it was all right for him in the end.' Vincenzo sat down beside her, and slipped his arm around her shoulders.

Suddenly the sight of Piero's things hurt her unbearably, and she buried her face in her hands. She struggled to fight the tears, but it was useless, and at last she cried without trying to stop.

'I loved him so much,' she wept against Vincenzo's shoulder.

'So did I,' he said sombrely, holding her tightly as much for his sake as hers.

'Stay with me here tonight,' she said. 'I want to remember him with you.'

He drew her down onto the bed that was only just big enough for the two them, and drew blankets over them.

She was still weeping and he made no effort to stop her. Sometimes he kissed her tumbled hair. Once he drew it back and stroked her face with tender fingers before kissing her gently on the mouth. She looked at him quickly.

'It's all right,' he whispered. 'Go to sleep. I'm here.'

She closed her eyes and he felt her relax. At last her breathing told him that she was asleep. He rested his head against her and had begun to drift off when she stirred and began to mutter.

'Julia,' he whispered, but then, 'Sophie.'

She gave a gasp that was almost a cry, and awoke.

'What is it?' he asked.

'It's a dream—it keeps coming back—'

'What happens in your dream?'

'It's about Annina.'

'You identified with her, didn't you? I can see why now. You loved your husband, and he shut you away for years—'

'And I died,' she said slowly. 'I died.'

'That's what you said, standing before her picture.'

She looked at him quickly.

'But how could you know that? It was only in my dream.'

'You were sleepwalking. You really went up there, and I came with you, just to see that you were all right.'

She searched his face. 'Yes, you did, didn't you?' she said. 'And you said you were my friend.'

'Do you remember anything else?' he asked anxiously.

'Yes.' She gave a faint smile. 'You kissed me.'

'That was the first time I ever kissed you, and you didn't know, not then or next day. I kept hoping you'd remember, but you looked through me.'

'Why didn't you tell me?'

'I couldn't. You needed to remember for yourself.' He grinned. 'I made good resolutions about waiting until the moment came.'

'You didn't keep them very long.'

'True. I'm not a patient man.'

'I'm glad of that.' She reached up and put her arms about his neck. 'I'm so glad of that.'

When he was sure he'd understood her properly he tightened his own arms about her.

'My love,' he said, 'let us drive the ghosts away. They have no place here now.'

'No,' she whispered, drawing him close. 'Not now.'

CHAPTER SEVEN

THE next day Julia left the *palazzo* for good, and moved into the little apartment over the restaurant. It consisted of one main room, and bedroom, with a tiny bathroom and even tinier kitchen.

New Year was almost on them, and she plunged into work, available at all hours, taking on any jobs, to keep her mind occupied.

'Don't overdo it,' Vincenzo advised one evening as she was just coming on for the late shift. 'You were here early, you helped with cleaning up all afternoon, and now you're starting work again.'

'I prefer to keep busy. The Montressis will be back soon. When New Year's over I'll try Murano again.'

'On your own?'

'Yes, but don't worry about me. If they're not there I won't fling myself melodramatically into the lagoon. I'll just keep trying until they are. I'll go as soon as Piero's funeral is over.'

It was Vincenzo who had paid for the funeral, arranging for Piero to lie beside Elena on the island of San Michele.

When the day came they both boarded the black motor boat that would take them across the lagoon. They made the journey standing up behind the black-draped coffin. Inside, Piero lay wearing the gloves, scarf and boots she had given him.

Soon the island came in sight, the outer rim of cypresses encased by a terracotta wall, and a few minutes later they reached the landing stage. Pallbearers appeared and carried the coffin onto dry land.

At the inner gate they were met by an official who checked the details with Vincenzo.

They were the only mourners. During the service she kept her eyes fixed on the coffin, topped by flowers from herself and Vincenzo. She had known Piero only a few weeks, yet she felt she had lost a very dear friend.

It was time to take the coffin to its final resting place. As they moved out of the chapel she could see that some of the cemetery was conventional, with burials in the ground, and headstones.

But this place had been created for economy of space, and most coffins were placed in narrow vaults, piled on top of one another, as many as ten high. At the outer end was a marble plaque giving the details of who lay there, with a picture. As there was also a holder for flowers a whole wall of these plaques was an impressive sight. Where two flowered walls faced each other the effect was of an enchanted bower.

Elena was on the fourth tier, her picture easily visible. She bore a marked resemblance to her father, having his sharp features and brilliant smile.

Slowly Piero's coffin was slid into the space beside her, and the end fitted into place.

'Goodbye,' she whispered. 'And thank you for everything.'

'I'd like to put some fresh flowers in my sister's urn,' Vincenzo said.

They walked along the long walls of flowers until Vincenzo stopped, pointing up at something above his head.

'That's Bianca,' he said. 'And the one beside her is her husband.'

Julia tilted her head back, but was unable to see the pictures clearly.

'How do you get up so high to change the flowers?' she wanted to know.

'There are some steps somewhere.'

He went searching around the corner and reappeared wheeling a set of steps high enough to reach the upper levels. Julia studied his sister's face and even from this distance she could see the family resemblance between them. There was a gentleness about Bianca that was instantly appealing.

'I didn't like him,' Vincenzo said, 'but she loved him. They only had four years together before they died.'

'Why didn't you like him?'

'He was too smooth a character. You can see it there in his face.'

She glanced up again, trying to get a better view of the man, whose face was partly obscured by flowers.

Suddenly she felt as though the very air about her had shuddered. She clutched the steps to avoid falling.

'What is it?' Vincenzo asked, concerned.

'I want to climb up.'

'Why? What's the matter?'

'I need to see more closely.'

Feeling as though she were moving through a nightmare, she began to climb the steps, her gaze fixed on the man's face as it grew closer. She took a deep breath, expecting it to change before her eyes. This must all be a terrifying mistake.

But there was no mistake. The face engraved in the marble was that of her husband.

She could hear Vincenzo's voice calling her from a great distance. Gradually the world stopped spinning and she realised that she was sitting on the steps, shivering violently.

'For God's sake, what's the matter?' he demanded, aghast. 'You nearly fainted up there.'

'It's him,' she said through chattering teeth.

'What do you mean?'

'My husband, Bruce. That's him up there.'

'Julia, you're overwrought.'

'I tell you, that's him.'

She forced herself to her feet. 'Let me see him again.'

'All right, and you'll find that it's just a chance resemblance.'

She climbed back to the top step and fixed her eyes on the man, almost hoping to find that it had been a mistake. But there was no doubt. It was the face she hated. Silently she went down and sat on the steps again, feeling as though she were turning to ice.

'That is Bruce,' she said slowly. 'How does he come to be here?'

'Julia, I think you're wrong. You haven't seen him for years and your memories are distorted by hatred.'

'I know what he looked like,' she said angrily. 'Oh, why was I stupid enough to lose his pictures overboard? If I still had them you could see for yourself. That's him.'

Vincenzo drew a sharp breath. If she was right the implications were so monstrous that for the moment he couldn't accept them.

'I can't get my head around this,' he said slowly. 'I know him as James Cardew. He came here five years ago.'

'Was he alone?'

'Julia—'

She clutched his hand painfully. 'Was anyone with him? Tell me.'

'He had a little girl with him,' he said slowly.

'How old?'

'About three.'

'Blue eyes? Fair hair, slightly ginger?'

'Yes.'

'That's my daughter. Where is she?'

'*Mio Dio!*' he whispered, appalled. 'How can this have happened?'

'*Where is she?*'

'Since they died she lives with me.'

'I must see her.'

'Wait!' She'd half risen and he seized her arms. 'It isn't as simple as that.'

'She is my daughter. I am her mother. What could be simpler?'

'But you can't just go up to her and tell her who you are. She thinks you're dead.'

She shook her head wildly. 'No, I don't believe you.'

'James told us that he was a widower. The child believed it. She's had years to get used to the idea. For her it's reality. Julia, please try to understand. You can't simply burst on her out of the blue.'

She leaned hopelessly against the side of the steps.

'I didn't believe I could hate him any more than I did,' she said. 'But he had one last trick up his sleeve.'

Other mourners were coming towards them along the tunnel of flowers. He helped her to her feet.

'Let's find somewhere else.'

They found a seat in the cloisters at the far end and sat quietly for a few minutes, both stunned by what had happened.

At last a harsh sound, part laugh, part sob, burst from her.

'I've dreamed of this for so long. It was going to be

the happiest moment of my life. Now I feel as if I've been punched in the stomach. You've got to admit that's funny. Oh, heavens, isn't it hilarious?'

She began to laugh softly, trying to smother the sound with her hands.

'Don't,' Vincenzo begged, slipping his arm around her.

'What shall I do? Cry?'

When he didn't answer she looked up and saw that he was looking back the way they had come, to where a middle-aged woman and a little girl had appeared before the plaques of Bianca and her husband. The woman was controlling a pushchair in which a child slept.

'Who are they?' she asked in a shaking voice.

'The woman is Gemma. I employ her as a nanny.'

'And the little girl?'

The world seemed to stop. He was looking at her with an expression of terrible sadness.

'Oh, my God,' she whispered. 'That's—?'

'Yes.' He was gripping her tightly now.

'Let go of me.'

'No. Julia, stop and think. She doesn't know you. She's grieving for the death of her parents.'

'They weren't her parents. Your sister wasn't her mother.'

'But she loved her as though she was. I'm sorry, I know this is painful for you, but for Rosa's sake you must listen.'

'Rosa? Her name is Natalie.'

'Not any longer. He told us her name was Rosa. She's forgotten Natalie.'

'Forgotten me, you mean?'

'I think he set himself to drive you out of her memory, yes.'

'And he succeeded.'

'It's been five years,' he said urgently. 'The child believes what she's been taught to believe. Think what the truth would do to her now. Don't force any more burdens onto her.'

'You're saying I'm a burden to her?' she demanded, aghast.

'You would be *at this moment*. I beg you to leave it until we've both had time to think.'

'Time for you to spirit her away where I can't find her,' she flashed.

He didn't reply in words, but the white-faced look he gave her was so full of shock that she backed off.

'I'm sorry, I shouldn't have said that.'

'No, you shouldn't,' he said harshly. 'Is that the sort of man you think I am?'

'How do I know? Once I thought Bruce was wonderful. When people are fighting over a child they do things that you wouldn't have dreamed—'

'Are we fighting? Have we ever fought? I think I've deserved better from you than that kind of accusation. But since you lump me in with all the others, *here*.'

He pulled a small notebook from his pocket, scribbled something and tore off the page with a gesture that was almost violent.

'That's where I live now,' he snapped. 'Come any time and you'll find her there. But think very carefully about what you're going to say to her.'

Without giving her a chance to answer he stormed off in the direction of the woman and child. Julia sat, frozen with dismay, shocked at herself for having said such a thing to him, appalled at the discovery that had made them almost enemies.

She watched the little scene in the distance. The woman had drawn the steps up to the wall of plaques, climbing them, then taking out the flowers. She descended and indicated for the child to climb up, with the fresh flowers she was holding. She mounted and began to place flowers in the urns, first her father's, then Bianca's.

She was coming down now, sitting on the steps in exactly the same spot where Julia had sat only a few moments ago. She wasn't weeping, merely crouching there with the stillness of despair. The woman tried to comfort her, but to Julia it was hard to tell if the child even noticed.

She felt as though a band were tightening about her heart. How well she knew that feeling of desolation, so deep that the slightest movement didn't seem worth the effort.

Then it swept over her in a tide of anguish. This child was grieving for the loss of her parents, of her mother.

Her mother! Not Julia. Not the woman who'd yearned over her through heartbroken days and agonised nights. *Someone else!*

Then the little girl looked up, saw Vincenzo and, with a glad cry, began to run towards him. He opened his arms and she hurled herself into them, babbling in Italian. Julia could just hear the words.

'I looked for you—'

'I'm here now,' he soothed her. 'But what are you doing here?'

'You said you were coming to the funeral of your friend, so I asked Gemma to bring me to see *Mamma* and *Papà*. I knew you'd come to see them too.'

Julia began to move forward very slowly, staying close to the wall, making no disturbance, but getting close enough to see better. Then the little girl raised her head from Vincenzo's shoulder, and Julia gasped at the sight of her. If she'd had any doubts before, they were settled now, for it was her own mother's face that she saw. This was the child she had last seen years ago, at the start of the nightmare.

Vincenzo looked back and for a terrible moment Julia thought he would ignore her. Instead he said gently, 'Rosa, I have a friend for you to meet.'

The child looked straight at her. Julia held her breath, waiting for the burst of joyful recognition.

But it did not come.

Rosa regarded her mother politely but without recognition.

'*Buongiorno,*' she said.

'*Buongiorno,*' Julia replied mechanically. 'I am—'

She fell silent. No words would come. She could hear her own heart pounding.

'This is Signora Julia Baxter,' Vincenzo said.

'*Buongiorno, signora. Sono Rosa.*'

She offered her hand. Hardly knowing what she did, Julia took it. For a moment it lay in hers. Her daughter had shaken her hand like a stranger.

Vincenzo was introducing the nanny, who had a kind face. Julia greeted her mechanically. She was functioning on automatic while her brain struggled to cope.

'Julia came with me to Piero's funeral,' Vincenzo explained. 'He was a friend we were very fond of.'

'I promised Carlo he could come to see *Mamma* and *Papà* this time,' Rosa said. 'He was too young before.'

'Carlo?' Julia asked blankly.

She knew that she sounded vague, but that was because her mind was rejecting the monstrous idea that was growing. Surely it was impossible?

But nothing was impossible.

'He's my little brother,' Rosa said, indicating the sleeping child in the pushchair. 'He's only two.'

She reached out eagerly to Vincenzo. 'Come with me.'

He took her hand and they went up the steps together. Julia heard her say, 'I didn't do the flowers properly.'

And Vincenzo's tender reply, 'Let's do them together.'

He helped her to arrange the leaves. When they had finished the child stood a moment looking at the pictures. Slowly she passed her fingertips over them as though seeking comfort from the cold marble, then leaned forward and kissed them, first her father, then her step-mother. Julia bent her head, unable to watch. But in the next moment she looked up again, unable not to watch.

She waited for her daughter to cry, but, as before, Rosa's face was blank. Whatever she was feeling was being kept bolted down and hidden from the world.

'Just like me,' Julia thought, appalled. 'I know exactly what's happening to her inside. But no child should feel like that, or have such a look of frozen misery. Dear God, what's happened to her?'

After a moment the little girl came down and went to the pushchair, gently shaking the toddler. He awoke with a gurgle, instantly smiling.

Like Bruce, Julia thought. He's got his face and his charm.

The nanny started to help but Rosa shook her head, polite but determined as she undid the straps and helped him out. Hand in hand they climbed the steps together.

'Look,' Julia heard her say. 'That's *Papà* and that's *Mamma*.'

He beamed and stretched out his hands to the faces of his parents, but when they encountered only cold marble he flinched back. Puzzled, he looked at his sister, and reached out again.

'Mamma,' he said. *'Mamma, Mamma!'*

He began to sob, pounding the marble with his fists and screaming out his disillusion.

At once Rosa gathered the child into her arms, murmuring soothing words.

'It's all right, little one. It's all right. We'll go home now.'

She helped him down to the ground, put him back into the pushchair and kissed him gently, stroking him until he stopped crying.

'It would have been better to wait until he was a little older,' Vincenzo told her.

Rosa nodded sadly. 'I'm sorry, Uncle Vincenzo. I just didn't want him to forget them. But I should have remembered he's only a baby.'

She turned politely to Julia.

'Buongiorno, signora,' she said, as politely as a little old lady. 'I'm afraid I must be going now. I hope that we will meet again.'

'So do I,' she said with an effort.

She watched as the little party walked away, the baby's hand extended to clutch Rosa's, as though there he could find safety.

'I didn't know they were coming here,' Vincenzo said. 'Rosa just spoke of the next few days.'

'That little boy—is he—?'

'Yes, he's Bianca's son, and James'. I wish it hadn't been sprung on you like that.'

'I suppose I should have thought of it.'

Suddenly the wind that blew down the corridor of flowers was bleak and desolate. She shivered.

'It's cold. I'm going home.'

The group had reached the end of the path and were

about to turn out of sight. They stopped and looked back at Vincenzo.

'We need to talk,' he said, 'but—'

'But you have to go.' She smiled faintly. 'Your family needs you.'

'You'll come with us to the landing stage?'

'I think I'll wait and take the next boat. Go quickly before they get worried.'

'Yes.' He was uneasy, but there was no choice.

Julia didn't watch him catch up with the others. She turned away and walked in the opposite direction, wondering how this could have happened. After the years of yearning and hoping she had finally met her daughter again, and the moment that should have been so happy had brought her greater pain than anything in her life.

Vincenzo didn't appear at the restaurant that evening. Julia tried not to read anything into it, but she regretted hurling an accusation at him. He was her only friend and it was foolish to alienate him.

But she knew that this practical reason wasn't the only one. Bit by bit the sense of closeness they shared had become essential to her.

She thought of him as the man she might have loved if love were not impossible for her now. Deeper than that she didn't dare to look into her own heart.

When the restaurant closed she went wearily up the stairs and shut herself in. Her brain felt as though it were going around and around on a treadmill. She must go to bed and try to sleep, but she knew she would only lie awake.

The building was old-fashioned, with shutters on the windows. As she went to close them for the night her gaze was caught by something in the *calle* below.

Pushing open the window, she leaned out and saw a man standing there.

'Come in,' she called.

She was at the door, waiting for him as he turned the corner of the stairs, ready to open her arms to him in her relief.

'I didn't think you'd come,' she said fervently.

He nodded almost curtly, but made no move toward her. 'I had to.'

'I thought you were angry with me after what I said.'

She stepped back to let him into the room, realising that there would be no embrace.

'No, I'm not angry any more,' he said. 'You were in a state of shock. Let's forget that it happened.'

This wasn't the joyful reunion she'd anticipated when she'd seen him in the street. He was here, but emotionally he was holding back from her in a way he'd never done before. When she laid a hand on his arm he smiled cautiously, but didn't take her into his arms.

'Perhaps you'd make me a coffee,' he said politely.

'Of course,' she replied, matching his tone.

As she was working in the kitchen he came and stood leaning against the doorway.

'I may even have deserved your suspicion,' he said. 'I wouldn't spirit her away, but for a moment I did wish I could turn the clock back, to before you appeared, and stop it happening. Rosa has been part of my family for five years. I love her. Do you think I wanted to admit that she's yours?'

'Does that mean that you're going to say that she isn't?' she asked sharply.

'I can't do that. I wish I could, but I did some checking on the internet tonight. I found several reports about the robbery, confirming everything you told me. One of them had a tiny picture of your husband, just good enough to show that he really was the same man as James Cardew.

'And the first time I ever saw you, that night Piero brought you home, there was something familiar about you. I didn't understand it, but actually I was looking at you and seeing Rosa.'

'But we're not alike.'

'Except for one thing—her forehead. She has exactly the same low forehead that you have. Usually her fringe hides it, but tonight I saw her brush the fringe back, and then everything became clear.'

They returned to the main room and he chose a single chair rather than the sofa where she might have sat beside him.

'I need to know more,' she said quietly. 'Everything you can tell me about him.'

'Does it really matter now?'

'I have six years of blanks to fill in. I won't like what you tell me, but I have to know.'

'Yes, I suppose you do,' he said at last. 'All right. I'll tell you everything I can.'

CHAPTER EIGHT

VINCENZO took a deep breath, and started.

'It seems as though your friends who thought they'd seen him in Venice and Rome were right. Bianca met him in Rome, where he was as an art dealer.'

'An art dealer?' Julia cried in disgust. 'But he knew nothing except what he learned from me.'

'He seems to have been a genius at presentation. Plus he had a lot of money and his premises were in the wealthy part of town.'

'That would be his cut from the robberies,' she guessed.

'Yes, it must have been enough to give the impression of success. When Bianca came home he followed her here. He said he was expanding, establishing a branch in Venice. The truth, as I later learned, was that he'd had to get out of Rome, fast. He'd sold some apparently priceless artefacts to a powerful family, who naturally wanted their money back when they turned out to be fakes.

'They sent people to Venice, who explained to James that, if he didn't pay up, bad things would happen to him. So he did, having no choice.

'After that, what money he had left ran out quickly. He was extravagant. He bought useless rubbish for show, made bad investments. He was a rather stupid, shallow man.'

'Yes,' she said. 'That's exactly it.'

'But there was nothing to make me suspect him of

worse than that. He had a passport in the name of James Cardew and hers said Rosa Cardew. He had a whole file of paperwork establishing that James Cardew was a successful art dealer with a list of grateful clients in several countries. Someone in the gang must have forged them for him before they parted company.'

'I don't think so,' Julia said. 'Otherwise the man who split on him could have given the police his new name. No, it must have been done later, by someone else. I dare say false documents are easy enough to get, if you have the money.'

'He certainly had money for a while. When it ran out he got desperate. He tried to get some out of me, although this was after the crash and the whole world knew that we had nothing. But he was sure I had some secret cache hidden from the creditors. He suggested that it was time I handed over Bianca's ''share''.'

'Yes, that was how his mind worked,' she remembered. 'He could never believe that things were exactly as they seemed, especially where cash was concerned. Did he think she had a secret fortune when they married?'

'He as good as admitted it. I don't think he married her entirely for love. Maybe not at all.'

It took her a moment to appreciate what he was saying, and then she turned on him.

'Is that supposed to delight me?' she demanded furiously. 'Do you think I care who he loved?'

'I don't know how you feel. You were once deeply in love with him.'

'That was in another life.'

He nodded wryly. 'I keep telling myself that things happened in another life. But it's odd how the lives overlap when you least expect it. Anyway, like a fool I borrowed against the restaurant for my sister's sake. She'd

had a rough time. I didn't want things to get worse
for her.'

'How long did it take him to come back for more?'

'Not long. This time we had a fight and he ended up
in the canal.'

'Good,' she said simply.

'The one good thing I know of him is that he honestly
seemed to love Rosa. In his way he was a good father.'

'A good father, after the way he separated her from
her mother, without a thought for either of them?'

'I only meant that he always showed her a lot of af-
fection, and interest. If she tried to tell him something
he'd stop what he was doing and listen, however long it
took. Lots of parents can't do that, however much they
love the child—'

'Yes, all right,' she interrupted him in a strained voice.
'You're right, he was a good father. I remember now how
he loved being with her.'

'And she adored him. She also came to love Bianca.
That's not easy for you to hear, but you have to know
what you're dealing with.'

'Thank you,' she said in a colourless voice. 'I couldn't
tell much from seeing her today.'

'No, she didn't cry or show any emotion, did she?' he
said heavily. 'It's been four months, and still—'

Julia stared. 'You mean she's never cried?'

'Not once. Even on the first day, when the news
came—' He broke off with a helpless shrug. 'She just
closed in on herself. She won't let anyone in, not even
me.' He looked at her. 'That's something you know all
about.'

'Yes,' she breathed. 'Sometimes it's the only form of
self-protection you have.'

'To pack your feelings away in an iron chest marked,

''No longer required''. Then bury that chest too deep to be found again,' he said, reminding her of her own words.

'But she's so young!'

'She's eight years old, but she's already lost three parents, and she can't talk to anyone about it. We all have our burdens but—'

'But hers are the worst,' Julia agreed sombrely.

'Normally she loves Carnival, but now she refuses to think of it.'

'Carnival?'

'In February. Everyone dresses up in masks and colourful costumes. Last year she had a wonderful time with James and Bianca. Maybe that's why she's not interested this year. I keep trying to entice her, telling her how excited she ought to be, but—' He shrugged.

'You can't get into someone's mind by force,' Julia said.

'No, I guess I know that.'

Suddenly she burst out. 'What am I going to do? Do you know how I've dreamed of the things I'd say to her when we met again? And now none of them will be right. What can I do?'

'You can trust me.'

'Can I?' she asked before she could stop herself.

He grimaced. 'I suppose you're bound to think that way.'

'How do I know what to think?'

He rose. 'Perhaps we shouldn't talk any more. We both have a lot riding on this, and we can't afford to quarrel.'

'In the meantime, I'm totally in your hands,' she said angrily. It was the kind of thing she'd resolved not to say, but she couldn't help herself. The strains of the day, the helpless sense of being so near and yet so far, filled her with tension that found relief in bitterness.

'I wish I could persuade you that you're safe in my hands,' he said.

'But you have my daughter and I don't,' she cried. 'How am I supposed to get past that?'

'Supposed to *forgive* that, you mean. Perhaps you never will. We'll talk another time.'

'When do I see her?'

'You have my address. All you have to do is turn up and bulldoze your way in.'

'You know I won't do that.'

'Right, because you're a good mother. That's what's holding you back. Not me.'

'And it'll always hold me back, won't it? It's what you're counting on.'

'Don't say any more, Julia. Don't say things that will make the future harder.'

She turned on him. 'Harder? How much harder than this can it get? Can't you understand what's happened? The last time I saw my child she clung to me and cried, "Mummy, no!" Today she—didn't even—recognise—me.'

The words came out in jerks. She was trembling violently, unable to prevent the sobs coming. They rose up in her, bursting out as gasping screams.

'Julia!' He came to her but she fended him off.

'No—no—keep away—I'm all right.'

'But you're not. At least let me help you.'

'How can you help me—when we're enemies?' she choked. 'That's true, isn't it?'

'No, we're not enemies. Perhaps we're on different sides, but you and I could never be enemies.'

'That's just words,' she flashed at him. 'If we're not

enemies now, we will be in the end. Don't you know
that?'

By his face she could tell that he did know it, however
hard he might try to deny it.

'No,' he said, trying to sound convinced. 'There's too
much between us.'

'There's nothing between us that matters,' she flashed.
'Nothing—nothing—'

She couldn't finish. The sobs were rising again, threatening to suffocate her. Vincenzo abandoned argument
and did what he should have done at first, putting his
arms around her and holding her tightly.

'Don't try to talk,' he murmured. 'Talking doesn't
help.' He sighed, resting his cheek against her hair. 'I
don't really know what does help, but it isn't words.'

She couldn't answer. Waves of grief overwhelmed her.
It was as if all the tears she had shed over the last few
years were still there to be shed again.

From somewhere she heard him murmuring her name,
and felt his head resting against hers. He was right.
Words were useless. The only comfort lay in shared
warmth, and it was only to be found in him.

'All these years,' she wept, 'thinking of her every day,
longing for her, loving her, but not knowing what she
looked like any more, dreaming of when I'd find her
again, what we'd say to each other—'

'I know, I know,' he whispered.

'What did I think was going to happen? Deluding myself—she was bound to have a new life—but I wouldn't
let myself see it—'

'Julia—Julia—'

'She doesn't want me.'

'It's too soon to say that.'

'No, it isn't. Don't you see I've been fooling myself

all this time? I'm a stranger to her. She doesn't want me and she never will.'

She wept without restraint. She had come to the end of the journey and the ending was bitter and hopeless. He tried desperately to soothe her, turning her face up to him and kissing it repeatedly. Her wretchedness tore at him and for a moment he would have done anything in the world to make things right for her.

Anything but the one thing she wanted.

He'd seen her face like this once before, the night she'd walked in her sleep and he'd promised to help her. How far away it seemed now.

He kissed her tears, then her lips, gently at first, then fiercely as though trying to call her back from some distant region.

'You said there was nothing between us,' he said huskily. 'But you're wrong. There's this—and this—'

For a moment she almost yielded. The feeling was so sweet and welcome. But now the distress that fuelled her whole life had extended to him, and she would not weaken.

'Yes,' she said wistfully. 'But it's not enough. Please, Vincenzo—'

He sighed and released her.

'You're right,' he said. 'It's not enough. I'd better be going.'

She wanted to say something to keep him there. She wanted him to go.

She longed to think of the right thing to say, but the words wouldn't come to her, and he was equally silent.

'Goodnight,' he said at last.

'Goodnight.'

He left, closing the door quietly behind him. Julia

could only stand, in violent despair, watching that closed door, wishing she could dash her head against it.

That night her dreams were haunted by a child screaming for the mother she was about to lose. She could feel the arms about her neck, desperately clinging on as she was torn away.

'No, Mummy, no!'

She awoke to find herself sitting up, staring into the darkness, clinging onto the wall as though to stop herself from falling.

After that she didn't dare go back to sleep. She got up and spent the rest of the night walking the silent *calles*.

She wondered what she would say to Vincenzo, but when she went to work there was no sign of him. Someone said he'd called to say he wouldn't be in today.

She made a decision.

'I'm due for a day off,' she told the head waiter, 'and I'd like to take it now. I'm sorry about the short notice—'

'It's OK, we're not too busy,' he said kindly.

She stormed out into the street and began to run in the direction of the Grand Canal. It was an unfamiliar route, but by now she was becoming a Venetian, and managed not to get lost more than once. When she reached the water she boarded a *traghetto*, one of the two-man gondola ferries that crossed the Grand Canal. Like the others she made the journey standing upright, huddling her jacket around her against the icy wind, and the snow that was falling again.

By studying a map she managed to identify the address Vincenzo had given her in the Fondamenta Soranzo. As she reached the shore she was already working out the rest of the way: down this *calle*, across that little bridge.

Suppose they weren't there? Suppose his disappear-

ance meant that he'd taken her away? Wherever they had
gone, she would find them.

There was the doorway, opposite her on the other side
of a small canal. In another moment—

*You're a good mother. That's what's holding you back.
Not me.*

The words seemed to leap out at her from the clear
air. Only last night she'd said she would not 'bulldoze'
her way in. And now she was doing it.

She watched the house for any sign of movement.
Slowly, she began to retreat into the shadows until she
turned the corner. Then she ran back the way she'd come
and almost jumped into the returning *traghetto*.

On the other side she jumped out again and headed
straight for the nearest art shop. There she spent money
in a fury, buying colours, pencils, brushes and pigments.
She finished off with a large, canvas artist's bag, stuffed
everything into it, and headed for the Palazzo di Montese.

As she came near she crossed her fingers, hoping that
she could still get in. There was the little back door. She
put her shoulder to it, giving it a push and a shake. It
opened.

'Trust you to know how to do it,' she whispered to the
unseen friend she still remembered.

Once inside she carefully closed the door and hurried
on upstairs. In the upper corridor she stopped and looked
up at the ceiling, where there were some frescoes that
had taken her attention before. Now that the light was
good she could see how really fine they were; also that
they needed her attention.

'I should have done this before,' she muttered.

Unlike most of the ceilings in the *palazzo*, this one
wasn't too high, and now she knew where to find a step-

ladder. She put it in place and shinned up, but was still not close enough.

A tall, empty bookshelf stood nearby. From the top of the stepladder she managed to scramble onto it. Lying on her back, she had just the view she wanted. The old, familiar excitement began to grow in her as she saw what time had done to the fresco, and knew what she could do to make it right.

So absorbed was she that she failed to hear the faint sounds coming from below. It was Vincenzo's voice that alerted her.

'Careful where you step. Take my hand.'

And then a child's voice, 'It's awfully big, Uncle Vincenzo. Did you and *Mamma* really used to live here?'

'We did once, when we were children. Did she ever tell you about it?'

'She did sometimes. She promised to bring me here, but *Papà* heard her and got angry. Why was that?'

'I don't know, *cara*. He had his own way of seeing things. Perhaps we shouldn't have come.'

'Oh, but you promised. I've been looking forward to it.'

'But it's a gloomy place, for you.'

'It wasn't always gloomy, though, was it?'

'No, my darling. Once it was full of lights and laughter. But that was a long time ago.'

Julia lay on top of the bookcase, unable not to eavesdrop, her heart beating fast at the sound of her daughter's voice. But Vincenzo's voice also caught her attention. There was no harshness in it now. It was gentle and tender as he spoke to the child.

They must just be on the stairs below, and she could hear him very clearly, talking about the old days in this place. Sometimes the little girl laughed, and then he laughed with her. They were delightful together. Julia lay there, high up, listening, torn between sadness and aching delight.

But she couldn't stay here, waiting to be discovered. Slowly she began to inch to the edge of the bookcase, from where she could get to the stepladder.

Nearly there—nearly there—one hand on the ladder—a few more inches—

But the ladder moved as she touched it. Grasping frantically, she somehow lurched back against the bookcase, and the next moment the whole lot came crashing down to the floor, with her underneath.

For a moment she lay still, trapped beneath everything, more winded than hurt.

She heard Vincenzo call, 'Rosa, come back here—' and the next moment the child came flying around the corner.

'*Uncle Vincenzo, come quickly.*'

He appeared a moment later, frowning at the sight, then exclaiming violently as he recognised her.

'It's the lady from yesterday,' Rosa cried.

'Julia, what the devil? *Julia!*'

'I'm all right,' she gasped. 'If you could just get this stuff off me—'

Instantly the child reached out tiny hands to the bookcase.

'Get back,' Vincenzo told her sharply. 'You'll hurt yourself.'

When he was sure she was clear he removed the stepladder, then lifted the bookcase and swung it right away.

'Don't try to get up,' he ordered Julia as she began to move.

'I'm all right,' she said decidedly. 'No bones broken.'

'Your forehead's bleeding,' Rosa said.

She touched it and found the trickle of blood. Then Vincenzo's arms went about her and he was helping her to her feet.

'Can you walk?'

'Yes, of course I—hey.'

He'd lifted her and was carrying her to the room that had been the count's bedroom. Rosa ran ahead and opened the door so that he could go through and lay her on the great bed. He pulled off his jacket and put it under her head as a pillow. Then he sat beside her, glaring.

'If you aren't the most—what the devil were you doing?'

'Looking at your frescoes.'

'Why?'

'It's about time somebody did. It's my job.'

'You have to do it here and now?' he demanded, astounded and exasperated in equal measure. 'No—wait—that can come later. You need a doctor.'

'I just had a little fall and a few bruises. But I could do with something to drink.'

'I'll get you some water from the pump. Rosa, stay with her. Don't let her get up.'

He left the room, and at once the child came to the bed, as though standing guard.

'It's all right,' Julia said. 'I'm not going to run away.'

'Good, because Uncle Vincenzo says you mustn't.'

'Do people always do what Uncle Vincenzo says?'

Rosa considered this seriously. 'Sometimes.'

'Do you?'

She shook her head solemnly. Julia wondered if she was imagining a gleam of mischief in the childish eyes. She would have liked to believe it was there.

'You're the lady I met yesterday, aren't you?'

Julia nodded.

'Why are you here?'

'I'm an art restorer.'

'Is that the same as an artist?'

'No, I was never much good as an artist, so I look after other people's pictures, and repair them.'

'Are you doing that for Uncle Vincenzo?'

'The truth is that I had no right to be here. I'm just nosy, I'm afraid.'

This admission seemed to strike a response in the child.

'Oh, yes, like when you're looking at a book of pictures and you've just got to keep turning over more and more pages.'

'That's it,' Julia said. 'The pictures are so beautiful that you can't get enough.'

'And you wish ever so much that you could make pictures like them,' Rosa said wistfully. 'But you just can't.'

Julia looked up quickly to see Vincenzo standing in the doorway. She hadn't heard him come in, and wondered how long he'd been there.

Rosa was full of eagerness.

'Uncle, this lady understands about pictures and wanting to look at them even though it's time to go to bed.'

Vincenzo grinned. 'We have constant battles about bedtime in our house.'

He brought a glass of water to the bed and offered it to Julia, who was hauling herself up painfully.

'Thank you,' she gasped, fumbling for the glass.

But it was Rosa who secured it, climbing onto the bed and directing Vincenzo to hold Julia up. He slipped his arms beneath her shoulders while the little girl held the glass to her lips.

'Can I have your hankie, please, Uncle?'

He handed over a clean handkerchief, and Rosa used

it to dab at the blood on Julia's forehead. Her little face was concentrated, as though this were the most important job in the world. Her hands were gentle.

'There,' she said solemnly at last. 'That will do until the doctor sees it.'

'Thank you,' Julia said as Vincenzo laid her back on the jacket. She smiled at Rosa. 'That's very kind of you.'

'I'm going to be a nurse when I grow up,' the child told her. 'Or I may be an art restorer. If I can read all the books in time. But it's hard because Gemma keeps telling me to put the light out and go to sleep.'

'I used to get into trouble for that too. My mother couldn't understand that, to me, an art book was as good as a thriller.'

Rosa nodded again, this time vigorously. 'What did you do?' she asked.

Julia leaned nearer, like a conspirator, and whispered, 'I got smaller books and hid them under the bedclothes.'

She winked. Rosa gave a little gasp, which almost turned into a giggle. Almost.

'Now can I ask what you're doing here?' Vincenzo said. 'Why didn't you just tell me, instead of coming here alone and climbing about in that dangerous way?'

'I did it on impulse. I thought it would give me something to think about other than—well, things I didn't want to think about.'

Out of the corner of her eye she saw Rosa grow suddenly still. It was an alert stillness, as though someone had blown a trumpet, and she was waiting.

'I expect you have a lot of things that you don't want to think about,' Julia said carefully.

Rosa nodded.

'But you can't stop,' she said.

'I know. The more you don't want to think of them,

the more you keep thinking of them, until it's like a great big stone crushing you. And you can't get out from under it.'

This time Rosa didn't nod, but a light came into her eyes, and she continued to watch Julia intently.

'I think I should get you back to your flat,' Vincenzo said. 'Then I'm sending for the doctor, and I want no argument. Nor are you coming in to work at the restaurant. You'll rest until Epiphany is over.'

'Then she can spend Epiphany with us,' Rosa breathed. 'Uncle Vincenzo, please say she can.'

Julia drew in her breath, waiting for Vincenzo to find some excuse.

'Will you feel well enough for that?' he asked.

'Yes, I know I will.'

'You'll come?' Rosa exclaimed. 'And stay with us all day?'

Julia glanced at Vincenzo. He was very pale, but he spoke steadily.

'Of course you will stay all day. So now you must rest properly, to make quite certain that nothing prevents you being our guest.'

'*My* guest,' Rosa said proudly.

CHAPTER NINE

IT SNOWED the night before Epiphany, but by the morning it had stopped, the sun was out, and Venice lay under a shining white blanket.

Vincenzo came to collect Julia and exclaimed, '*Mio Dio*, what are you carrying?'

'Gifts for Rosa. After all, it's her day, isn't it? Piero told me that Italian children hang up their stockings now, not at Christmas.'

'You'd better let me take some. There was no need to load yourself down like a donkey.'

'Six missing birthdays. Six missing Christmases. I'm making up for all those times I wasn't able to watch her face as she opened things. She won't know, but I will.'

As they walked through the snow she said, 'By the way, how did I become Signora Baxter?'

'It was the first name I could think of. Do you mind?'

'No, it'll do. I'm so happy today I'd agree to anything.'

She gave a little skip in the snow and he had to grab her to stop her slithering. They laughed together and now he could hear the different note in her voice. She had come back to life. The next moment she broke free and began to pelt him with snowballs. He dropped the parcels and pelted her back.

As it was a feast day there were no *traghetti* crossing the Grand Canal, so they walked over the Accademia Bridge. Halfway across Julia stopped and looked down the length of water to where it broadened out into the lagoon, flashing and gleaming like a million swords in the sunlight.

'If people knew Venice was as beautiful as this in winter, nobody would come in the summer,' she said.

'You're turning into a Venetian,' he teased.

'I reckon I am.'

She gazed ecstatically up into the sky, which was a brilliant blue.

'I can't believe this is happening,' she breathed. 'After all these years I've seen her again, I'm going to spend the day with her and she likes me. Not as a mother—it's too soon for that, I know. But she likes me, *she likes me.*'

'Steady,' he said, taking her shoulders. 'Try to keep your feet on the ground.'

'No, why should I?' she said, laughing. 'I don't want my feet on the ground. The ground's so hard. Believe me, I know. I've slept on it.'

He gave her a gentle shake. 'Julia, you're crazy.'

'Yes, I'm crazy,' she cried joyfully. 'I'm crazy with happiness, crazy, *crazy!*'

Some passers-by looked at her, but instead of scuttling past in alarm they grinned, falling in with her mood. This was Venice, where crazy people were the norm.

Just the same, Vincenzo took the precaution of kissing her firmly before she could say any more.

'Will you shut up?' he begged between kisses.

'Maybe. Persuade me.'

He kissed her again and again, feeling her young and glorious in his arms, wishing it could always be like this. He took her face between his hands, looking deep into her eyes. But although he saw his own reflection there he knew that was only on the surface. Behind that surface was something else that excluded him.

'Julia,' he said, trying to call her back to him. *'Sophie.'*

'Whatever. What does anything matter? I thought I'd never have even this much again, and I'm going to enjoy today. I'll worry about the rest later.'

Now he could see her as she'd been years ago, young and full of hope, before grief and despair had marked her. He grinned and told her something that would please her.

'You heard what Rosa said about your being *her* guest? Because she was the one who invited you. She's determined to do all the entertaining herself. She even wanted to cook the meal, but I drew the line at that. Gemma cooked it, but she'll be leaving as soon as we get there, to spend the day with her family.'

'You should have let her cook it,' Julia declared. 'It would have tasted glorious.'

'I've tasted Rosa's attempts at cooking,' he said darkly. 'Believe me, it would probably have poisoned you.'

'I wouldn't care. Isn't she a wonderful little person, Vincenzo? Did you notice what she did that day in the *palazzo*, when I had that fall?'

'You scared the life out of me.'

'But not out of her. She wasn't scared, although it must have sounded like a terrible crash down where you were, and I heard you tell her to come back, but she didn't take any notice—'

'The little monkey never takes any notice,' he said, unable to keep the fond pride out of his voice.

'She just dashed up bravely. It could have been anything making that racket, but all she cared about was finding out. She's one of those people who runs forward to life with her arms out. I'm so proud of her already, aren't you?'

'Yes, I am—'

'*She's wonderful,*' Julia carolled up to the sky.

He gave up trying to remonstrate, knowing that she was beyond reason. Nor did he really want to bring her down to earth. Something caught in his throat at the sight of her joy, and he wished it could last for ever.

'We should hurry,' he said. 'Gemma can't leave until we get there.'

'Then let's go,' she said, seizing his hand and pulling him off the bridge, determined to be delayed no longer. Soon they reached the Fondamenta Soranzo, where her eyes sought the windows of the house.

'Look, there's Rosa, watching for us,' she cried, and waved eagerly.

The little girl waved back, beaming. Vincenzo opened the front door into a large hallway, with a flight of steps leading up.

'We live up there,' he said.

'Uncle Vincenzo!' called a child's voice from upstairs, and the next minute Rosa came flying down to envelop him in a fierce embrace.

Then she turned her attention to Julia, too. But immediately she stood back and became the perfect hostess, polite and formal.

'*Buongiorno, Signora Baxter.* I am very pleased to welcome you to this house and I hope you will have a very happy day with us.'

'Thank you, I know that I will,' Julia said, charmed. 'But please call me Julia.'

'Signora Julia.'

'No, just Julia.'

Rosa cast a quick glance at Vincenzo, who shrugged and indicated Julia, saying, 'It's for our guest to decide.'

'*My* guest,' Rosa insisted. 'Because I invited you.'

'Yes, you did, and it was very kind of you,' Julia said, smiling.

The sun had come out. Her daughter was a charming child with generous, confiding ways, and she had reached out to her.

'Come with me.' Rosa seized her hand and drew her up the stairs, Vincenzo following.

The apartment was spacious and attractive. The main room contained furniture that looked antique and had probably come from the *palazzo*.

Rosa took her coat and ushered her to the sofa, then bustled busily away. Julia heard her speaking to someone in the next room, then Gemma emerged, wearing an outdoor coat, and bid everyone goodbye.

In the centre of the room was a low table on which stood several plates, bearing cakes and biscuits, some elegant glasses, and a bottle of *Prosecco*. Rosa reappeared and began to pour some of the sparkling white wine for Julia and Vincenzo and orange juice for herself.

'Please have a cake,' she said to Julia. 'Lunch will be in an hour.'

'Perhaps I'd better look after the final stages,' Vincenzo said. 'Why don't you show Julia your presents?'

Rosa promptly became a child again, bouncing to her feet and drawing Julia into the next room where there was a decorated tree, and signs of gifts opened with eager fingers. Rosa showed them off proudly.

'I should really have waited for you to come before I opened my presents.'

'Never mind,' Julia told her. 'When I was your age I always got down to business very early, usually about six o'clock on Christmas morning. In England children hang up their stockings at Christmas, not Epiphany.'

Rosa was wide-eyed. 'You don't have Befana?'

'I'm afraid I don't know what that is.'

'Befana is a kindly witch. They say the three kings invited her to visit the baby Jesus with them, but she was busy and didn't go. Later she changed her mind, but by then she'd missed the star and lost her way. So now she flies around on her broomstick and leaves presents in every house where there are children, because she doesn't know which house is the right one.'

'That sounds lovely. I'm glad you told me about her. Now I know who it must have been.'

'Must have been?' Rosa queried.

'This old woman who whirled around my head on her broomstick, and dropped something into my bag. She said she hadn't delivered everything to this house, and didn't have time to come back, so would I bring a few things for her?'

As she said this Julia produced her gifts. She had spent much time choosing them in an art bookshop, asking for 'Something for a *very* intelligent eight-year-old.' The sight of Rosa's face as she unwrapped everything told her that she'd chosen well.

'You remembered,' Rosa breathed.

'Yes, I remembered what we said the other day,' Julia agreed, 'but I also remembered myself when I was your age. These are the kind of things I loved to read.'

She fell silent, watching as Rosa examined one book that she'd chosen with particular care. It was almost entirely pictures, each one with a large caption that was repeated twice, once in Italian, once in English.

Rosa ran her fingers down one of the shiny pages, letting them rest on the English. She was frowning a little, but then she nodded and looked up, smiling.

Julia reached into her bag. 'And I brought this for

Carlo. I didn't wrap it because I thought perhaps you should see it first and make sure it's all right.'

It was a magnetic fishing puzzle. There was a brightly coloured picture, showing jungle creatures against lush foliage. Each animal could be separated from the background by dint of dangling a magnet until it made contact.

Rosa let out a whoop. 'He'll love this.'

'I hope so. The shop said it was suitable for a two-year-old. It's supposed to develop his skills at—well, moving and co-ordination and that sort of thing. Oh, never mind that. It looks fun.'

'Oh, yes, it does. Carlo will love it.'

'I remembered how sad he seemed the other day, and I thought he needed cheering up.'

'You saw him at San Michele, didn't you? Uncle Vincenzo was right, I shouldn't have taken him. He thought he was going to see *Mamma* and *Papà* and when they weren't there he cried. But you see—' She hesitated.

'Please trust me,' Julia said. 'You can tell me anything. I won't repeat it.'

Rosa nodded. 'My mother died when I was the same age as Carlo, and I can't really remember her. And I hate that. It's like having a gap when there ought to be somebody. I didn't want that to happen to Carlo, but I got it wrong.

'He's too young to understand about people dying, you see. He only knows that there's something missing. So Uncle Vincenzo and I show him lots of extra love. Gemma does too, of course, but we're his family. And that's different.'

'Yes,' Julia said slowly. 'Family is different.'

'Do you have any family?'

'I—no.'

'None at all?'

'My parents are dead.'

'And you never got married?'

'Well, yes, I did, but he's dead too.'

'No little boys or girls?' When Julia didn't answer Rosa was immediately contrite. 'I'm sorry, I didn't mean to be rude. Please forgive me.'

'You weren't rude,' Julia said huskily. 'I did have a little girl but I—lost her several years ago. She would have been about your age now.'

Rosa didn't answer in words, but she got up from the floor where she was sitting and put her arms about Julia's neck. Julia hugged her back, overwhelmed by the feel of her child's warmth and her cheek pressed against her own.

'I'm sorry,' Rosa whispered.

She drew back and smiled directly into Julia's face.

'It would be nice to think she would have been like you,' Julia said.

A glint of mischief came into the child's face. 'You wouldn't like it really. Uncle Vincenzo says I'm a fiend.'

'Oh, does he? And are you?'

'Oh, yes. I'm the worst fiend who ever, ever lived.'

'Hmm. That sounds final enough. I guess you must be.'

As she spoke her eye was caught by a large photograph on the sideboard. It was a wedding picture, the bride in glorious white satin and lace. Vincenzo, looking younger, stood beside his sister.

Just behind it was another picture, showing the bride and groom with a little girl in front of them, and in another the bride stood alone, holding the child in her arms. They were regarding each other fondly.

Julia drew a sharp breath. For all her euphoric mood

there would still be such moments to be faced. Rosa had
been three when these pictures had been taken, and re-
cognisable as the baby Julia had lost. Now she was nest-
ling in the arms of another 'mother'. Unconsciously Julia
tightened her own arms around her child, as though by
doing so she could reclaim her.

'That was you,' she said softly.

'Oh, yes, when *Mamma* and *Papà* got married.'

Julia forced herself to let go. 'Do you have any more?'

'There's an album here,' Rosa said, diving down the
side of the bookcase.

Vincenzo appeared in the doorway, saying, 'I'm just
going to check on Carlo, see if he's awake yet.'

'I'd better come too,' Rosa said at once.

'I can be trusted to look after him,' he complained.

'Yes, but—he likes to see me when he wakes up,' Rosa
said seriously, and hurried out of the room.

Vincenzo sighed. 'She's just like her mo— Like
Bianca. She thinks nobody else can be trusted to do anything. We won't leave you alone for long.'

When they had gone Julia began to go through the
album Rosa had given her. She knew the contents would
hurt, but she had to learn all she could.

It was full of pictures of Bianca and Rosa: more wedding shots, then every milestone in the child's life, birthdays, Christmas, Epiphany.

There was the child in her father's arms, snuggling
against him with an air of content. On this evidence he
looked like a good father.

And he really did love her, she thought. That's why
he took her with him instead of leaving her with my
mother. What am I going to tell her when the time
comes?

'Come along,' said Rosa's voice from the doorway.

She was holding Carlo by the hand, leading him forward until they were both standing before Julia. He was the image of his father.

'Say *"Buongiorno"*,' Rosa told him in a stage whisper.

But the little boy hid his face against her and shook his head vigorously.

'He's shy,' Rosa said. 'Look, little one, here's a present for you.'

But he only shook his head the more and began to grizzle, clinging onto his sister.

'I'm sorry,' Rosa said, lifting him in her arms. 'I'd better take him back. He'll be better later.'

She hurried out with the weeping child. Vincenzo, who had been watching, said in a low voice, 'While we have a moment, there's something I need to know, although I have a horrid feeling I know the answer. If your husband simply vanished I don't suppose there was ever a divorce?'

'Not that I heard of.'

'So he was still married to you when he married Bianca. *Bastardo!* And Carlo is illegitimate. You've seen how it is with him and Rosa. He's one of the things that's holding her together.'

Something else linking her to her new life. Something else taking her away from her mother.

'Julia—'

'It's all right,' she said, shaking her head. 'I've got my breath now.'

She rose and went in search of Rosa. Hearing a murmur from behind a door across the hall, she followed the sound and found herself in a room with a bed and a cot. The two children were sitting on the floor.

'May I come in?' she asked tentatively.

Instead of hiding, the little boy giggled at her. Encouraged, Julia sat down on the edge of the bed.

'He doesn't mind me?' she asked.

'No, he's all right here,' Rosa explained, 'because this is our room. Befana brought him lots of presents this morning. Look.' She swept out a hand towards a merry pile. 'But this one is still his favourite, even though it's years old.'

She pointed to a blue furry rabbit that the boy was clutching, so old and shabby that much of its fur was gone. As Julia looked a strange feeling began to come over her, part ache, part joy. She had seen that rabbit before, long ago, in another life, when it was bright and new.

'Yes, it looks very old,' she said slowly. 'Who gave it to him?'

'I did,' Rosa said proudly. 'His name is Danny. He was my best friend when I was young.' She spoke as if she were a hundred. '*Mamma* said that when we met I was clutching him and I wouldn't let him go. *Papà* was ever so cross.'

'Wh—why?' Julia asked in a shaking voice.

'He didn't like Danny. He kept trying to throw him away.'

Of course he did. Because he knew I'd given you that toy just before we were parted, and he wanted to wipe me out of your mind.

'When you say he *kept* trying to throw him away—'

'He did it again and again. *Mamma* kept rescuing Danny and giving him back to me. It's funny that she understood when *Papà* didn't.'

'She sounds nice,' Julia said carefully.

'She was lovely. She used to get cross with *Papà* because he wouldn't write home to the family and try to get some pictures of my mother.'

'*She* did that?'

'Yes. She'd ask me if I remembered my real mother, but he stopped her. I heard them arguing. He said *she* was my mother, but she said a real mother was special and nobody could take her place.'

So Bianca had been generous and kind. Julia felt a moment's gratitude to her, mingled with pity that she too had come under Bruce's spell.

'I don't think *Papà* liked my mother very much,' Rosa went on. 'He didn't keep any pictures of her, and he wouldn't talk about her. If I asked him, he always started talking about something else.'

'You don't have any pictures of her at all?'

'No,' Rosa said wistfully. 'I don't even know what she looked like.'

'You can't remember anything?'

'Oh, yes, odd things. She used to hold me close against her, and she smelled lovely. And she laughed all the time. I remember her voice too, not the words because I didn't understand them, but the way she spoke. She loved me. I could hear it.

'But I can't see her face. That's why it would be nice to have some pictures of her and me together, and it would be real again. Because she was real, and yet she wasn't. Like a ghost really. If I saw her I wouldn't recognise her.'

'Yes,' Julia whispered. 'I know what you mean.'

Carlo made a small sound, demanding attention. Rosa took charge, arranging his arms more firmly around the elderly rabbit.

'Danny looks like a good friend,' Julia said.

'He's always been *my* good friend,' Rosa confirmed.

'But now he has to look after Carlo. I've explained that to Danny, so that he doesn't think I don't love him any more.'

'That was clever of you,' Julia said. 'Some things need to be explained in case people—or rabbits—misunderstand.'

Now she knew why Vincenzo had said the baby was keeping Rosa together. She had become his mother, responding to his needs and forgetting her own, feeding him, encouraging him.

She lost me at the same age, Julia thought. She knows exactly what to do for him.

And suddenly she saw herself, not as a mother alone, or a mother bereft, but as a mother in an eternal line of mothers, all loving a child more than themselves, whether or not it was their own child, and ready for all the sacrifices.

Whatever those sacrifices might mean.

CHAPTER TEN

WHEN it came to serving lunch Rosa was in her element, taking charge of the kitchen, blithely disregarding the fact that Vincenzo was a restaurateur, and reducing him to the status of a waiter. Julia watched in amusement as he meekly obeyed her orders.

As the guest of honour she was served first and received constant attention. The meal was excellent, and she solemnly thanked her hostess.

'I was there too,' Vincenzo said, aggrieved.

'Yes, you were very helpful,' Rosa told him kindly. Behind her hand she told Julia, 'Actually Uncle Vincenzo did quite a lot.'

'Thank you, ma'am,' he said, catching her eyes and grinning.

She grinned back. Carlo joined in the laughter, banging his spoon on the table, and Julia laughed from sheer happiness.

Afterwards Rosa put Carlo down for his nap while the others got on with the washing up.

'I must take my hat off for the way you're coping,' he said.

'I've had to take a few deep breaths, but I'll be blowed if I let anyone know that.'

'Except me. Or don't I count?'

'In a way you don't,' she mused, not unkindly, merely reflecting. 'You already know the worst of me.'

'I know the best, too.'

She turned to him eagerly. 'Vincenzo, listen, something wonderful happened. Do you remember that rabbit I told you about, the one I bought her a few days before we were separated?'

He nodded. 'It's Danny, isn't it? I thought so as soon as I knew who you were. I remember the first time I saw her. She was clutching it tight. Her father didn't like that.'

'Yes, she told me. She also said that your sister kept rescuing it. She seems to have defended my right to be part of my daughter's life, despite everything he did to blacken me.'

'He cast you in a bad light whenever he could. I suppose he had to, in order to explain why he had no contact with your family. But, as you say, Bianca defended you.'

He stopped quickly as Rosa came back to say that Carlo was sleeping. She spent the next hour going through the books Julia had bought her, showing them to Vincenzo and carefully explaining any points that he might find too difficult to understand. Julia watched him with fascination, liking the way he didn't talk down to the child.

After that Carlo woke up and they all played magnetic fishing. Carlo went at it with great energy and crowed with delight whether he succeeded or not. Vincenzo was unaccountably clumsy, while Julia and Rosa, both equally dextrous, went head to head in a hard-fought challenge.

'I think that's a draw,' Vincenzo said at last through his laughter as the two competitors solemnly shook hands.

The phone rang. Yawning, he answered it.

'Gemma! Are you having a good day? Oh, I see—yes, it's a tough situation—you'd better stay. Don't worry, I can manage. I'll just take my orders from Rosa. *Ciao.*'

He hung up. 'Gemma's elderly mother is feeling poorly and she wants to stay there tonight.'

'Lovely!' Rosa bounced with joy. 'Now Julia can stay with us. I'll make up the bed in Gemma's room.'

'Rosa,' Vincenzo said hastily, 'you're supposed to ask our guest what she wants to do, not just mow her down with a bulldozer.'

Rosa turned astonished eyes on Julia. 'But you do want to stay, don't you?' she asked in a puzzled voice. 'I mean, you don't really want to walk home alone in the cold and dark.'

'She wouldn't be alone,' Vincenzo said. 'I'd walk with her.'

'No way,' Julia said. 'You can't leave Rosa and Carlo here alone.'

'No, I can't, can I?' he realised.

'You see?' Rosa said triumphantly. 'And you don't want to do that walk alone, do you? Because it's terribly cold and terribly dark and you might fall into the water and you wouldn't like that.'

'I might even get lost and that would never do. It's very kind of you to ask me.'

'That's all right, then.' Rosa bustled away.

Julia choked with laughter, barely able to meet Vincenzo's eye.

'It looks like you're stuck with me,' she said.

'Oh, we've both been given our orders. She's a very assertive little character.'

'She always was,' Julia remembered. 'Even when she was Carlo's age she was strong-willed.'

'I wonder where she gets that from,' Vincenzo said wryly.

'No, you don't. You think you know.'

He grinned. 'It may have crossed my mind.'

'I'd better go and help Rosa.'

Together they put fresh linen on the bed in the snug little room. The look Rosa gave Julia was brim-full of delight.

We could be a family, she thought as they settled down for tea. I'm dreaming and if I pinch myself I'll wake up. But I don't want to.

Nothing happened to spoil it. A lull fell on the evening and they watched cartoons on television until it was bed-time.

Rosa departed with Carlo, then came back in her py-jamas.

'Carlo wants you to say goodnight to him,' she said, taking Julia's hand.

But they found him already asleep. Despite her efforts she felt her eyes blur as time shifted back to another dimly lit bedroom, another two-year-old, sleeping in per-fect trust and confidence.

'Goodnight, my darling,' she whispered, leaning down to kiss his cheek. Suddenly she couldn't resist adding the words she had always said, all those years ago. 'Angels keep you.'

'What did you say?' Rosa asked quickly. 'It sounded like English.'

'Yes, it was English. I don't suppose you understand that, do you?'

'Not very well, but I've started English lessons at school. The teacher says I'm the best in the class.'

Of course you are, she thought, because English was your first language. At two and a half you knew three hundred words, and the last words you cried out to me were in English.

Rosa hopped into bed and held out her arms. Julia hugged her fiercely.

'Say it to me too,' Rosa begged as she lay down to be tucked in.

'*Buonanotte, mia cara. Speroche gli angeli ti custodiscano.*'

'No, like you did before, in English.'

'Goodnight, my darling. May the angels keep you.'

She kissed her child, and sat there holding her hand until Rosa went to sleep. Even then she sat there, brooding, full of joy and sadness.

At last she backed quietly out of the room, and closed the door.

As she returned to the main room she could hear the phone ringing again, and then Vincenzo speaking in an angry, impatient voice.

'Look, don't call me at home, and especially during Epiphany. Don't you people have any families? I've told you before, the answer's no, and it's going to stay no. Goodbye!'

He hung up firmly.

'Well, that's telling them,' Julia said, going in and settling herself comfortably on the sofa.

'Someone wanting to buy the *palazzo* for a hotel,' he growled. 'It's like trying to swat flies. Kill one and there's a dozen others.'

'Piero once told me that you were dead set against it.'

'That's putting it very mildly indeed.'

'It's a pity. It would make a wonderful hotel.'

'Are you out of your mind? Sell my home?'

'Of course not. *You* turn it into a hotel.'

'Using what for money?'

'You get investors. Why not? Look at the Danieli. It started its life as a *palazzo*, in the fourteenth century.'

'That's true.'

'Put yours to use. Bring it back to life. Isn't that better than letting it fall into ruin?'

'It's already doing that.'

'So put a stop to it now. There's still time to restore it before things get worse.'

'Ah, now I see. You're touting for business. Mind you—it's an idea.'

'I don't know why you've never thought of it before.'

'Because I'm the world's worst businessman. All I saw was fending off the sharks who thought I was desperate enough to sell at a knock-down price. I just wanted to make enough money from the restaurant to keep my head above water, but that's not enough, long term.'

'No, and the best way to beat the sharks is to steal their ideas. You'll have your home back, not as it was, but more than you have now.'

'People don't live like that any more,' he mused. 'Not in the modern world. They either go into business, or the place goes under.' He smiled. 'Maybe it floods when there's nobody there to protect it.'

She nodded, smiling back at him.

'I'm getting dangerously light-headed,' he mused. 'You're filling me with crazy ideas and they're beginning to sound sensible.'

'Of course. I'll be your first backer.'

'Have you got any money to invest?'

'Not money. These.' She held up her hands. 'I'll renovate the frescoes for nothing, and that will be my stake. You'll have to do the place up and get some suitable furniture. It might be best to open it a wing at a time, and move the restaurant in there almost at once.'

'And what about the pictures that were sold?' he demanded. 'Even with investment I couldn't buy them back. Or do we open with bare patches on the walls?'

'Of course not. You put up copies, which is what you'd have to do even if you had the originals. The insurance company would insist.'

'And you're going to knock me out some copies, are you?'

'Certainly. I do a mean Veronese, and my Rembrandt is even better, although I must admit my Michelangelo isn't so hot.'

'Your—?'

'But we can put those in a dark corner and people won't notice. And don't forget you still own some pictures, stored upstairs. You can either hang them or use them to raise more cash.'

The words were pouring out now as the excitement of the idea gripped her. For a moment she was all artist and planner. Vincenzo regarded her with wry admiration.

'You've got everything worked out, haven't you?'

'Not at all. It came to me this minute, because of that phone call, but now it's all becoming clear.'

'Wait, I can't keep up with you.'

'You don't have to. Just say yes to anything I say, and leave the rest to me.' She added unnecessarily, 'I'm a very organised person.'

'So tell me what we're going to do.'

'We're probably not going to do anything,' she said regretfully, 'but if we were I'd say you ought to start making plans. It'll be Carnival soon—'

'In a few weeks. It'll take a year before we could open—'

'I know that, but you could have a big party there during *this* Carnival, and make a press announcement.'

'A party,' he mused. 'We used to have great Carnival parties there when I was a boy. Such costumes, such outrageous masks!' He gave a sudden grin, full of sensual reminiscence. 'If you only knew the things we did!'

'I think I can imagine. All behind the safety of the masks, of course.'

'Of course. That's what masks are for. When it all started, hundreds of years ago, masks were forbidden the rest of the year. But in the last few weeks before Carnival anyone could hide their face, become someone else, and do as they pleased. Then you had all of Lent to fast and be good, and generally make up for it. The tradition lasted.'

'And did you usually have much to make up for?' she teased.

'Well—' he said in a considering tone. 'A moderate amount.'

'Hmm!'

'Perhaps a bit more than that. When you're a young man—' He stopped with the air of someone choosing his words carefully.

'Go on,' she encouraged.

'Let's just say that self-restraint wasn't considered a virtue.'

'I suppose being a Montese helped.'

'Nonsense. With the mask on, nobody knew who I was.'

'Oh, yeah?' she said with hilarious cynicism.

'Well—maybe.' Again there was the grin, recalling days of delight, before the crushing burdens descended.

'I'll bet the girls were queuing up halfway across St Mark's Square.'

He looked offended. 'What do you mean, *half*way across?'

He stared into his glass of red wine, seeing it all there,

the whirling colours and wild faces, the dangerous freedom and the dangerous use he'd sometimes made of it.

He'd loved that sense of wonderful things about to happen, but it had gone from his life, fading away down the winding alleys, like his outrageous youth.

Only once, recently, had he recaptured that feeling: in the darkness of a hot, sweet night with a woman in his arms who had maddened and intrigued him from the first moment. She had made love to him with a fervour and abandon that had startled even while it had thrilled him.

Afterwards he had told himself that she was his, and it was the biggest mistake he had ever made. But for those few riotous hours he'd known that she belonged in Carnival, beautiful, secret, unpredictable.

'Your face gives you away,' Julia said, watching him.

That startled him. 'What am I thinking?'

'You're remembering your wild youth.'

'Well—yes, but there was a bit more to it than that.' He looked at her leaning back against the cushions, her eyes bright.

'I wish I'd known you then.'

'You might not have liked me. I was a bit of a hooligan, the way young men tend to be when they have too much money and are too much indulged. You know what happened to my family. The fact is that when the crash came I wasn't very well equipped to cope. Too spoiled. Too used to my own way.'

'What happened to your fiancée?' Julia asked, trying to sound less interested than she was.

'She married a man with pots of money. Our engagement party was a Carnival event, with everyone dressed up to look like somebody they weren't—which is ironic, if you think of it.'

'Do you still mind about her?'

He shrugged. 'It's so far away that I can't remember what it felt like to love her. I was another person. You know that feeling.'

She knew it well. Wisdom told her to drop the subject now, but for some reason she couldn't let it go.

'Piero told me how she came down the grand staircase, looking wonderful, and you stood there—'

'Probably with a fatuous expression on my face,' he said. 'I should have seen then that it was the staircase and the surroundings, plus the title, that she really wanted. She just had to marry me to get them. When they weren't on offer any more—' He shrugged.

He gave a brief laugh. 'I suppose in my heart I always knew the truth, but I wouldn't let myself believe it. When she dumped me so fast it was a surprise, and yet it wasn't, if you see what I mean.'

She nodded.

'I'd like you to see one of those Carnival parties,' he said.

'Well, maybe I will, if our idea comes off.'

'Oh, suddenly it's *our* idea?'

'But it's a *good* idea. Vincenzo, after what happened to you, you seem to have got your life back together, but actually you're treading water. It's time to go on to the next thing. Get your home back, and as soon as it's even partly habitable, you, Rosa and little Carlo can take up residence.'

'And what about you?'

'I'll be there, not in expensive rooms because we'll need them for paying customers. I'll just have a tiny place, and we'll meet for business discussions.'

'You mean you'll stay a ghost?' he challenged her. 'You came in the night, now you plan to haunt the fringes of my life?'

'Hardly the fringes, since we'll be living under the same roof. It's the best thing for Rosa. I'll be around when she needs me. She and I can see each other every day, but I won't be intrusive. You say I'll be a ghost, but maybe that's right for her. She's at ease with ghosts, haven't you noticed? She knows some of them are friendly.'

'And is that the best we can ever hope for?' he asked in a low voice.

'I don't know. You once said you'd like to turn time back until before we met. If you did that, I'd be wiped out too, wouldn't I?'

'I didn't mean that,' he growled. 'Do *you* understand your own feelings about everything? I wish I hadn't met you *like this*. It might have been so different, but who knows where the road leads from here?'

'Some day—'

'Some day—when one of us has turned the other's life upside down.'

'Yes, we can't get past that, can we?' She sighed. 'The rest is a happy dream, and dreams can only last so long.'

'But you know better than anyone how long dreams can last,' he said. 'As long as you have the courage to make them. Let's keep ours while we can, forget reality and think about us. I know, I know—' He silenced her with his fingertips across her lips. 'Who can tell if there'll ever be an "us"? But can't we pretend, just for a little while?'

She tried to murmur, 'Yes,' but he silenced her again, this time with his lips. The touch of them answered all questions. For a few precious moments there was no other reality but the one to be found in his arms.

When he rose and held out his hand to her she went with him, smiling. As they passed through the dark hallways he held her close, burying his face against her neck, her hair, telling of his desire in whispered tones that made the hot eagerness spread through her like fire.

'*Mummy!*'

The sound ripped through the air, piercing them, driving them apart.

'*Mummy, Mummy, no!*'

It came from behind Rosa's door and it was followed by a long, despairing wail. Julia was through the door in a moment, putting on the light.

Rosa was sitting up, her eyes closed, her arms outstretched as if in a desperate plea, tears pouring down her face, lost in some terrifying nightmare. Julia sat on the bed and pulled her into her arms, hugging her tightly until the little girl awoke.

'There, darling, there, darling.' She was talking English although she didn't know it. She was aware of nothing except the need to soothe and comfort the child.

Rosa was awake now, sobbing violently, clinging onto her. Vincenzo went to Carlo, who'd been roused by the noise, and picked him up. His face was haggard.

At last Rosa's weeping subsided, and she lay with her head on Julia's shoulder, hiccupping slightly. Julia drew back and looked down into the tear-stained face, trying to believe what she had heard. The child's words had been so like that other time. Surely it wasn't possible—?

'What happened?' she asked, remembering to speak in Italian this time. 'Did you have a bad dream?'

'Yes—I think so—it was cold and dark and I was frightened.'

'Can you remember anything else?' she asked, trying not to let her voice shake.

Rosa frowned for a long time, but at last she shook her head.

'It's just dark, and I'm feeling scared and—so lonely and unhappy. It's like—the worst thing in the world is happening, but I don't know what it is.'

'Do you—remember what you called out?'

'I don't think I said anything. I just screamed and screamed.'

She searched Julia's face in sudden anxiety. 'Did I say anything?'

'No,' Vincenzo said in a tense voice. 'You didn't. You just made a lot of noise and scared us both to death, you little rascal.'

His voice had become teasing, telling her everything was all right, warning Julia to probe no further.

The warning was needless. Not for the world would she have pushed her child faster than she was ready to go. Tonight she'd been shown a ray of hope, and she would live on that.

'Do you want some hot milk?' he asked.

Rosa nodded contentedly, resting her head against Julia again.

'Can you get it, please, Uncle Vincenzo? I want Julia to stay.'

He laid Carlo back in his cot and went out to the kitchen.

'Do you get nightmares often?' Julia asked gently.

'Sometimes. Since my parents died. But they're all confused and muddled up and afterwards I can never tell what they were about…'

Her voice trailed off and after a moment Julia realised that she had gone to sleep again, contented now. She sat stroking the tousled hair, brooding over her child with fierce, protective joy.

After a while she laid her down, and Rosa half opened her eyes, whispering, 'Is Carlo holding Danny?'

'No, he's on the floor.'

'Can I have him?'

Julia picked up the shabby old rabbit and tucked Rosa's arms around him. The child gave a small grunt of pleasure, and was asleep instantly.

Julia slipped to her knees beside the bed and knelt there, holding one of Rosa's hands, watching her with loving eyes that missed nothing.

Vincenzo, coming in a moment later, found them like that, and went silently away without being observed.

CHAPTER ELEVEN

GEMMA returned next morning, and Vincenzo walked home with Julia. Rosa would have come with them, but Vincenzo gently discouraged her. This was their first chance for a private conversation since the events of the night before.

She had remained with Rosa a long time, emerging to find that Vincenzo had gone to his room. That had been a kind of relief. What would they have said to each other?

Now they walked in silence until Julia said, 'I feel as if I'd got to know Bianca, with Rosa's help. I'm glad. She's real now. And I have to deal with her.'

'Deal with her? How?'

'By accepting her. I suppose I had some idea of driving her out because she was usurping my place, but I can't do that. There has to be room for all of us. Rosa will only turn to me if she can bring Bianca with her.'

'Does that make you hate my sister?' Vincenzo asked in a low voice.

'No, I'm grateful to her. She did me no wrong. She looked after my child, and made her happy. Rosa says that Bianca actually defended me when her father tried to wipe me out. She wouldn't let him do it.'

'She was the most generous woman alive,' Vincenzo said sadly.

'Yes, I know that now. She tried to do me justice, and I'll do her justice.'

'And in the end Rosa will turn to you,' Vincenzo said. 'And you'll take her away.'

'Are you saying you'd just stand back and let me?'

'I won't stop her being with her mother, if that's what you mean. It has to be her choice, but you're going to win. We both know that. The affinity is there. She feels it. Deep down inside that child knows who you are. She doesn't understand what she knows, but it's there, and sooner or later it will come to the surface.'

'It nearly happened last night,' Julia said. 'She was crying out in English.'

'How can you tell? No is the same in both languages.'

'But she cried "Mummy" not *"Mamma"*.'

'Yes,' he said heavily. 'She was reliving that moment, but when she woke up she didn't remember. Next time—'

'It's a lot for her to take in,' she said placatingly. 'It might be a while yet.'

She wondered at herself for denying the very thing she most longed for, but, intentionally or not, he'd reminded her that they were on opposite sides, and she wanted to comfort him for the loss he was facing.

As the restaurant came in sight, still closed up, they saw a young man standing outside, trying to peer through the windows.

'Hallo,' Vincenzo called.

The young man jumped. He was thin, fair-haired and awkward-looking.

'Hallo?' he said. 'I'm Terry Dale. I work for Simon and Son. I'm looking for Mrs Haydon.'

'That's me,' Julia said at once. To Vincenzo she added, 'They're my lawyers in England. I called them when I moved in here.'

'Let's go inside,' Vincenzo said, opening the door to the restaurant and ushering them both in.

'I came because I've got good news about your compensation,' Terry Dale said when he was inside.

'I thought it was far too soon for the compensation to be settled,' Julia said.

'Normally, yes, but now that the conviction's been quashed, they want this one off their plate fast. They've made a generous offer.' Conscious of Vincenzo's unmoving presence, he scribbled something on a scrap of paper and thrust it at her. 'How about that?'

Julia's eyes opened wide at the sum.

'Are you sure you didn't add on an extra nought by mistake?' she asked.

'Good, isn't it? But that's not all. Everyone knows you've been looking for your husband, and if you've got any leads—well—'

'It's been years,' Julia said carefully. 'He may not even be alive any more.'

'That doesn't matter. Even if he were dead the police could track back and find out who he's been associated with, interview anyone he's known, that kind of thing. It could be worth quite a bit more to you.'

'I didn't know it worked like that.'

'Officially it doesn't, but this kind of information can help—'

Terry Dale was scribbling more figures, showing them to her like a puppy appealing for a pat.

'I don't like this,' she said. 'It looks like some people still think I'm in cahoots with him.'

'Oh, no, but they know you're looking for your daughter, and when you find her it'll help us get onto his trail. Like I say, it could be worth a lot of money to you.'

'That's too bad, because there's no help I can give,' she said firmly. 'I can't point you in the direction of my husband, and you can take that as final. The lesser compensation will have to do.'

'Well, it's a pity because—'

Julia picked up the paper with the figures and tore it again and again.

'Goodbye, Mr Dale. Please thank your boss for his efforts and ask him to finalise matters.'

She saw him out and turned to find Vincenzo regarding her with a look that was half appreciation, half suspicion.

'I didn't see the figures,' he said now, 'but it must have been tempting.'

'Oh, yes? And have police swarming all over the place, upsetting Rosa? No way.'

Inwardly she was cursing Bruce. Was his malign influence going to spread over the whole of the rest of her life, blighting everything?

'I've made my decision,' she said, 'and now I know where I'm going from here.'

A light had come on inside her. Vincenzo was reminded of the night she'd returned from Murano, ablaze with confidence and decision.

'What are you going to do?'

'First, give up my job as soon as you can do without me.'

'Right now if you like. Celia's due back from honeymoon.'

'Can I stay in the apartment for a while?'

'Sure. She won't be moving back in. But what are you going to do?'

'Get in practice at my job. Hone my skills again before I start on your place.'

She thought for a moment before adding, 'There's one thing I'm grateful for, and that's that the Montressis were away. If they'd been there I might have stirred things up in a way I'd be regretting now.'

'He's lucky they never bumped into him,' Vincenzo observed. 'They might have recognised him.'

'Not really. I don't think he'd seen them for years. They were only very distant relatives, but I pinned everything on them because they were all I had. Well, I won't need to bother them now. I'm just going to get to work.'

In prison she'd done some drawing, and even taken an art class for other prisoners, but now she needed sustained work to bring herself back up to standard.

Taking sketch books and charcoal, she began to walk around Venice the next day, making rapid strokes, creating life on the paper.

At first she took in the showplaces, St Mark's, the Rialto Bridge, but then she turned away into the little canals, the *calles* with washing strung overhead, the empty boats bobbing in the water. The outlines were easy, but when she'd mastered them there was the more tantalising task of evoking the atmosphere of those mysterious little places.

Absorbed in this challenge, she took a while to realise that she wasn't alone. A small but determined ghost was flitting just behind her, always vanishing if she turned her head, but then emerging again in determined pursuit.

'All right,' she called at last. 'Come out where I can see you.'

A figure, swathed up to the eyebrows in scarves, and down to the ears in a thick woolly hat, emerged from around a corner and presented herself. Julia folded her arms, regarding her wryly. The figure immediately folded her own arms.

'Are you following me?' Julia asked.

A nod.

'Is anyone with you?'

A shake of the head.

'You've run away on your own?'

The eyes were as mischievous as the voice. 'I'm not on my own. I'm with you.'

Rosa pulled down the scarf, revealing a cheeky grin.

'Uncle Vincenzo let me come to the restaurant with him today. He said you were upstairs so I was going to go up, but then I saw you leaving by the side door. So I followed.'

'Does anyone know where you are?'

'Yes. You do.'

'I don't think that's quite enough,' Julia said, trying not to laugh, and pulling out her cell phone. In a moment she was through to the restaurant.

'Vincenzo? I've someone here who needs to talk to you.' She held out the phone to Rosa. 'Talk.'

Rosa giggled and began her persuasion.

'I ran after Julia, and she says I can spend the day with her—'

'I said no such thing.'

'But you were just going to, weren't you? I can, can't I, Uncle?'

'Give that to me before you land me in trouble,' Julia said, hastily seizing the phone. 'Vincenzo?'

'I'd only just discovered that you're both gone,' came his harassed voice.

'Vincenzo, if you're thinking what I think you are, I'll never forgive you.'

There was a silence.

'I wasn't thinking that.'

'Really?'

'I wasn't thinking that you'd run off with her,' he said tensely.

'You'd better be sure about that.'

'Is she all right?'

'Of course she is. She's having the time of her life laughing at both of us. You'd better let her stay with me officially, otherwise she'll just creep after me at a distance. Don't worry, she's safe with me.'

She couldn't resist adding, 'Whether I'm safe with her is another matter.'

At this Rosa gave a giggle that clearly reached Vincenzo down the line.

'I'll say yes—having no choice. But you'd better put yourself in her hands. She knows Venice better than you do.'

Julia hung up and turned to her daughter. 'We're going to have a great time.'

Rosa gave a brilliant smile, took her hand, and they wandered on together.

'What did you think Uncle Vincenzo was thinking?' Rosa asked.

'It's a long, complicated story,' Julia said hastily. 'I'll tell you another time.'

After that the child said little, simply seeming to be content to be in Julia's company. And it was she who chose the next object to draw, pointing at an ornate bridge.

Julia promptly took out her sketch book, sat on a small flight of steps, and began to work rapidly. When she'd finished she showed the result to Rosa, who gave her an impish look, took the book, flipped over a page, and began to make a sketch of her own.

With disbelieving pleasure Julia looked at the result.

'You can draw,' she breathed.

Another page, another rapid sketch, drawn with an inexperienced but confident hand. Beneath a quiet surface Rosa was already a boldly confident artist. This was truly her daughter.

'*Papà* didn't like me drawing,' she confided. 'He said it was a waste of time. But *Mamma* said I should do it if I wanted to. It was our secret.'

'She was—' Julia checked herself and started again. '*Your mother* was right.'

The words were hard to say, but she felt she owed Bianca that much.

After that, wherever they stopped, they shared the drawing. Julia showed the little girl some new strokes, and had the delight of discovering a responsive pupil. It was a perfect day.

But then something happened that was like the sun going in.

As they moved closer to the glamorous heart of the city she noticed that almost every street had a shop that sold wild, colourful masks for the coming Carnival. Several times she would have stopped to look closely, but Rosa always pulled her on.

'Hey, stop a minute,' Julia begged at last.

Rosa stopped obediently and stood beside her, looking into the window. But she said nothing.

'They're for the Carnival, aren't they?' Julia said.

'That's right.' Just the two short words, almost snapped out.

'It's quite soon, isn't it?'

'Next month.'

'I've seen pictures, of course—people in those incredible costumes—it must be so exciting.'

'Yes, it is.'

Julia turned her head uneasily to look at the child, conscious of something strange in her replies. Her delight of only a few minutes ago had been abruptly quenched. Now she spoke like a robot, and her face was stiff.

Then Julia remembered Vincenzo saying, 'Last year she had a wonderful time at Carnival with James and Bianca, but this year she refuses to think of it.'

Silently calling herself a fool, she said, 'Why don't we go and have something to eat?'

Rosa nodded and followed her to a little café.

When they were seated with milk shakes she said, 'I'm sorry. I didn't think. It's your parents, isn't it?'

Rosa nodded. After a moment she said, 'I had a costume with lots and lots of colours last year, but this year I wanted a pink satin one. So *Mamma* bought it for me last July. She said we'd keep it for the next Carnival. Only then—'

She stopped. She was controlling herself almost fiercely, but her lips trembled.

'And you don't want to go without her?' Julia asked gently.

'I won't ever go again,' Rosa said, calming herself at last. Now her voice was too controlled, too unyielding.

Julia took a risk.

'I think you're wrong,' she said. 'If *Mamma* bought that lovely pink dress for you, then she'd want you to wear it, for her sake.'

'But she won't be there.'

'No, but you can think about her, and you'll know that you're doing it for her.'

'But that won't bring her back, will it?'

'It'll bring her back in your heart, which is where it really matters.'

Rosa didn't answer this, but she shook her head stubbornly. The impish confidence was gone, replaced by a stark misery that was all the worse because she felt that nobody really understood.

'Let's go back,' Julia said gently. 'Vincenzo will be worrying about us.'

The sun had gone from the day and a dreary rain had begun to fall. They found Vincenzo at the door, looking for them.

'What is it?' he asked as soon as he saw Rosa's face.

In a quiet voice Julia explained. Instantly Vincenzo put his hands on the little girl's shoulders, searching her face tenderly.

'Hey there, *piccina*,' he said. 'Have you been crying?'

She shook her head. 'I just remembered what you said—about how everyone leaves you.'

'What?' he said, aghast. 'Rosa, I never said that.'

'Yes, you did. You said it to someone at *Mamma* and *Papà's* funeral. I overheard.'

'But I—' Vincenzo checked. What use was it to say that he hadn't known she was listening? '*Cara*, I was feeling terrible, and that's the sort of thing people say when—when—I didn't mean it.'

'Yes, you did,' she said quietly, looking him straight in the eye. 'And it's true. People leave you even when you plead and plead with them not to.'

Her voice faded. She was staring into the distance.

'Darling—' Julia put a hand on the child's shoulder, but Rosa didn't seem to notice. She was lost in an unhappy dream.

'Even if it's the most important thing in the whole world,' she said, 'and you're trying to make them understand and begging and begging them not to go—they still go—and they don't come back.'

Suddenly she looked straight at Julia, who drew in her

breath. Did she imagine that those childish eyes contained a hint of accusation?

Then the moment was gone, and Rosa was looking bewildered.

'I think we should go straight up into the warm,' Julia said.

Upstairs they thawed out with the help of hot drinks sent up from the restaurant. Rosa began to seem more cheerful.

'Do you live here alone?'

'That's right.'

'Can I come and visit you?'

'Whenever you like.' She noticed Rosa's eyes closing. 'We walked a long way today. Why don't you take a nap?'

She tucked the child up in her own bed, where she fell asleep almost at once. Julia sat beside her for a while, free at last to watch over her with loving possessiveness.

You're mine, she thought. If only I could tell you.

Terry Dale called her a week later. Things were moving fast.

'The sooner you can get over here to sign the papers, the sooner you'll have the money,' he said.

'Fine, I'll be right there.'

'What about Rosa?' Vincenzo asked when she told him. 'Have you thought that your going away might worry her?'

'Yes, and I've got a plan. If I'm quick she need not even know I've gone. She's back at school now, and you said she has a good friend who often invites her for sleepovers. If you can get her invited for a couple of nights I can be there and back before she knows it.'

A few days later he told her the plan was in progress.

'She'll go home from school with Tanya tomorrow,' he said, 'and stay for two nights. Can you be back by then?'

'I'll manage it.'

'I've promised her you'll have dinner with us tonight.'

It was a good evening spent eating, laughing and watching television. The shadow had gone from Rosa's manner and she seemed free from the ghost that had briefly haunted her.

Julia promised to come to dinner again when Rosa returned from her visit, and the child went to bed, content.

'And what about me?' Vincenzo asked as he walked home with her. 'Do you promise me that you'll come back?'

'Don't be silly. You know I'm coming back.'

'Sure, you'll return for Rosa's sake. You heard what she said. Everyone leaves you in the end.'

'But that's what *you* believe,' she reminded him.

'Only because I've been proved right so often.'

'Trust me,' she said, echoing the words that he had said to her so many times.

'Shall I take you to the airport tomorrow?' Vincenzo asked.

'No, thank you. I have something else to do first.'

She refused to tell him any more. Next day she left, heading, not for the airport, but for San Michele. Before boarding the boat she bought flowers.

In the cemetery she went first to Piero's grave, and used half of the flowers to refill his urn.

Then she went to find Bianca. Pushing the steps into place, she climbed up, removed the wilting flowers from the urn, and replaced them with fresh ones. For a long time she looked at the sweet face of the woman her daughter called *Mamma*. Then she touched it gently.

'I just wanted to say thank you,' she said.

Julia's trip went well. She signed papers and received a cheque for the first part of her compensation, the rest to follow soon.

There were more questions about her husband, but she smiled and played dumb, and in the end her inquisitors gave up.

On the day of her return to Venice she was at the airport long before she needed to be, only to find it shrouded in fog. Passengers were allowed to board, pending an improvement in the weather, but it did not happen and they were requested to leave the aircraft.

Two hours later she called Vincenzo on her cell phone.

'I'm going to be late for dinner tonight,' she said. 'There's a thick fog and the planes are grounded.'

'There's no fog at this end,' he said, frowning.

'Well, it's a pea-souper over here.'

'How do I explain to Rosa? She doesn't know you're in England.'

'Make some excuse. Say I'm not well. Say anything—'

There was a whistling sound in her ear as the line went dead. The phone needed a top-up. While she was looking around for somewhere to do it a voice came over the tannoy.

'Will passengers for Venice please start boarding—?'

'Thank goodness,' she breathed. 'Oh, why did this have to happen?'

Vincenzo turned to see Rosa watching him, very pale.

'She's not coming, is she?'

'*Cara*—'

'I heard you say she was in England. She's gone right away and she's not coming home.'

'Yes, she is coming home, but her plane's been delayed by fog. She'll be here as soon as she can.'

'You didn't say she was going away to England.'

The sight of her rigid face shocked him. This wasn't simply childish disappointment. She was reliving an old nightmare.

He dropped down so that their eyes were on a level, trying desperately to find a way past her defences. It was like trying to communicate with someone behind bars.

He was assailed by a feeling of danger. If he couldn't reach her, and get her to reach out to him, she might be behind those bars for ever.

'Julia only went for a couple of days, to get things sorted out in England so that she can come here for good. We didn't tell you in case you were upset, and she's coming home quickly.'

Rosa shook her head. Her eyes were blank.

'No, she isn't,' she said.

He could have wept. If the child had been upset he'd have managed to cope, but her calm acceptance was ominous.

'You'd better talk to her yourself,' he said, hoping the noise he'd heard on Julia's phone didn't mean what he feared. But when he dialled he heard the same noise again and ground his teeth.

'She needs to top it up,' he said in despair.

'Perhaps she won't bother,' Rosa said.

'Of course she will. Why wouldn't she?'

She didn't reply, but her eyes revealed what she really believed: that Julia had blanked them out, and it was convenient for her phone not to work.

'She's probably boarding the plane right now,' he insisted. 'That's why she can't do anything about her phone. We'll hear from her when she lands.'

There was a touch of pity in the little girl's eyes. Why couldn't he face facts?

'Can we have dinner?' she asked. 'I'm hungry.'

'She'll be here,' he said, despairing.

'It's all right, Uncle. Honestly. You were right. People always leave you.'

'*Cara*, I wish you'd forget I ever said that.'

'But it's true.' Then, in a strange voice, she said, 'I begged her not to go—but she did—and she never came back.'

It was as though a phantom had flitted past, chilling the air for a moment before it vanished.

'Who are you talking about?' he asked, barely able to speak.

'Let's have something to eat,' she repeated.

'Rosa, who were you—?'

But it was useless. The phantom had gone. He let the subject drop, fearful of doing damage if he persisted.

For the rest of that evening she behaved normally, even cheerfully. You had to know the truth, he thought, to recognise the storm she was suppressing. Nor could he help her, because she wouldn't let him.

He kept hoping that Julia would find a way to call them soon. But the evening passed with no word from her, and at last it was time to go to bed.

He was awoken in the morning by Gemma, shaking him urgently.

'I can't find Rosa,' she said.

He threw on his clothes and checked every room in the apartment, but it was a formality. In his heart he knew where she had gone.

'Has the phone rung?'

Gemma shook her head.

'All right, I'll be back soon.'

He called for a water taxi and reached the nearest land-ing stage just as it arrived.

'The airport, as fast as you can,' he said tersely.

He entered the terminal at a run and kept on running until he saw Rosa sitting, watching the arrival doors with terrible intensity.

She glanced at him as he sat beside her, and something in her face silenced all words of reproach.

'How long have you been here?' he asked quietly.

'A couple of hours.'

He looked up at the board. It showed two planes landed from England, but he didn't know if either of them was Julia's.

'She'll be here,' he said. 'She promised.'

There was no reply, but he felt a small hand creep into his and grip it so tightly that he winced with pain.

The doors slid open. Passengers were beginning to stream out. Rosa's gaze became fixed again, as if her whole life depended on this moment. Vincenzo too watched, trying to distinguish one figure from the many others.

But it was Rosa who saw her. Leaping up with a sud-den shriek, she began to run.

'Mummy—Mummy—Mummy!'

Heads turned as the child darted through the crowd to throw herself into a pair of open arms. With a heart over-flowing with relief, Vincenzo followed her until he was a few feet away from Julia, and was in time to see Rosa draw back to look her radiantly in the face and say, *'You came back.'*

CHAPTER TWELVE

'You came back.'

'Yes, darling. I always meant to, it was just the fog.'

But Rosa shook her head, impatient that Julia hadn't understood.

'You didn't come back before,' she said.

Then the first inkling of the truth came to Julia and her startled eyes met Vincenzo's.

'Before?' she asked cautiously, hardly daring to hope.

'You went away before,' Rosa cried, 'and you never came back.'

Julia dropped to her knees, holding onto Rosa and searching her face.

'Do you remember that?' she whispered.

Rosa nodded. 'You gave me Danny, and then you went away. And I cried. I didn't want you to go, but you went.'

'Do you know—who I am?'

'I—think so,' Rosa said slowly. 'I think—you're Mummy.'

'Yes, darling. Yes, I am—I am, *I am*—'

She buried her face against Rosa and wept tears of joy, feeling them sweep away all the other tears she had cried through so many bitter, anguished nights.

'But I don't understand—' Rosa said.

'I know, *piccina*—this is your mummy,' Vincenzo said. 'There'll be time to understand later. Let's all go home.'

He took charge of Julia's trolley, and wheeled it out of the airport, glancing over his shoulder to see where they were following, walking slowly because they were hugging each other at the same time.

He helped the boatman with the suitcases, noticing that Julia had managed to acquire several new ones, and that they were heavy. By the time they caught up, everything was ready for departure.

He sat in the front, leaving them together in the back, just sitting, holding hands, not speaking through the roar of the engine, simply content in their discovery. As they sped across the water he wondered where the future led. He had only to glance at the faces of the mother and child in the back to know that each of them had all they wanted.

At last the boat came to a halt in the Fondamenta Soranzo.

'You need to be here tonight,' he said in answer to Julia's look of surprise.

While waiting for Julia's arrival he'd already called Gemma to say that Rosa was safe, so they arrived to find the apartment empty, Gemma having taken Carlo shopping.

Vincenzo assigned himself the role of cook and waiter, plying them with breakfast while they looked at each other in their new light.

'Why did you go away?' Rosa asked sadly. 'You left me, and you never wrote or sent cards, and *Papà* said you were dead—' Her voice shook.

Until this moment Julia had never quite decided how much she would tell Rosa when the time came. To speak of prison and her father's betrayal seemed terrible. But now she saw that the child was carrying a burden that crushed her, the belief that her mother had callously abandoned her.

'I had no choice, darling,' she said softly. 'They put

me in prison for something I didn't do, and then your father took you away. I didn't know where you were, but I never stopped loving you, and as soon as I could I came looking for you.'

She knew she'd judged right when she saw the load lift from Rosa's face. Her mother had not, after all, walked away from her. Nothing really mattered beside that.

Rosa noticed Vincenzo carrying Julia's things upstairs.

'Are you coming to live with us now?' she asked, thrilled.

'I'll be here tonight, and we can talk all we want. After that—'

After that—what? She sought Vincenzo's face for some sign of what he was feeling, but his features revealed nothing.

'You can have my room,' he said.

'That's very kind of you, but you—'

'I'll be fine.' He almost snapped out the words. 'It's time I was getting to work. I've neglected it a bit recently.'

'I'm sorry about what I did,' Rosa told him. 'I mean, running off. But you see—'

'Yes, I do see,' he said, ruffling her hair. 'But we were very worried about you. I'm so glad you're safe. Now I must go.'

They didn't see him for the rest of the day. For Julia it was a happy time, spent with her daughter, exchanging memories, feeling the bonds assert themselves.

'I always knew there was something about you,' Rosa confided. 'I didn't know what, but I knew you weren't just anyone.'

Vincenzo telephoned to say that he'd contacted Rosa's school and arranged for her to have a few days off for them to be together. But he hung up before Julia could thank him.

Late that night she waited up for him to return. There were so many things that she wanted to say to him too, if only he would be here. She resisted the thought that there was something ominous in his choosing to be absent.

As the hours passed she went to bed and lay awake, listening, longing for him. Now her heart reached out to him as never before as she understood the full extent of his generosity. He'd known from the start that he would lose Rosa as he had lost almost everything else. But he had put no barriers between them. On the contrary he'd done all he could to help the two of them rediscover each other, whatever the cost to himself.

She wanted to see him, hold him, and pour out her feelings now that the road was clear for them at last.

Eventually she heard the front door, then his footsteps. Throwing on a dressing gown, she went out to see him, and found him making up the sofa.

'You can't sleep there,' she said aghast. 'It isn't long enough for you.'

'It'll do for tonight.'

'But tomorrow—' Surely there was some way to say that his bed was big enough for two, if they squeezed in tightly. But why did it need saying?

'I've made arrangements for tomorrow. There's a tiny hotel just opposite. I've taken a room there.'

'A hotel?' she echoed, aghast.

'It's just on the other side of the canal. You can see it from here.'

'But when will I see you?'

'I'm not the one you need to see.'

'What about all the things we need to talk about?'

'Such as?'

There was no encouragement in his manner and so, instead of what she wanted to say, she blurted out, 'Money.'

His face seemed to close against her. 'Go ahead. Talk about money.'

'Now I've got my compensation I can invest some money in our hotel. And I've got the name of an Italian firm that goes in for this sort of thing. My lawyer in England has some international connections and he says these people are very good, completely trustworthy. Here.'

She handed him a scrap of paper, and he studied it before saying briefly, 'I've heard of them. They have a good reputation. Have you been in touch?'

'Certainly not. This is your show.'

'Really?'

'I only obtained their name,' she said indignantly. 'You said yourself that you're the world's worst businessman.'

'All right, all right.' He held up his hands as if fending off a swarm of bees.

It was going all wrong. Why didn't he take her into his arms and make everything perfect? Why couldn't he apparently see that now they were free to love each other? Unless he didn't want to see it.

'You'd better get back to bed,' he said. 'I'll sleep pretty well here. Goodnight.'

'Goodnight,' she said despondently, turning away to the door.

'Julia.'

'Yes?' She turned back, heart beating with hope.

'Thanks for all you've done—about the money and the hotel and everything. Goodnight.'

'Goodnight,' she said again, and closed the door behind her.

Vincenzo listened to her go into his room, cursing under his breath, wondering what was suddenly wrong with him.

Why should such an apparently simple thing have become so hard? She stirred his blood and his heart more than any woman had ever done, including his faithless fiancée. And what could be more natural than to ask her to be his wife?

But the words had frozen in him because he couldn't dismiss the picture of her face when she'd said it was better to use people than trust them. He closed his eyes, trying to blot out the memory, but it was replaced by another one: Julia saying, 'I'll do what I have to—whatever that might be.'

And if he could obliterate her voice and her expression, there was another memory that could never be dismissed because he could still feel it in his flesh: their first night together when she had loved him with wanton abandon, taking him on, challenging, demanding, giving, with a desire that was as fierce as it was dazzling.

Only afterwards, when he knew her story, had the niggling questions come.

Me? Or was I just the man in her bed when her need was great?

'Better to use people…' She had said it.

He wanted to shout a denial, to say she wasn't like that. But, as she'd so often told him, he knew nothing of her true self: as little, perhaps, as she did herself.

Today she had reclaimed her daughter's heart, but there were still matters to be sorted out. Not just living arrangements, but the child's attachment to himself and her baby brother.

For Julia, their marriage would make solid, practical sense. If he proposed now, she would say yes but he wouldn't know why. They would set up home with the children, the perfect picture of a happy family.

And he would never be quite certain of her or her love, as long as he lived.

The next day Vincenzo discovered the reason for Julia's numerous heavy suitcases. Somehow, in a mere two days, and in between dealing with lawyers, she'd found the time to buy up half the clothes shops in London.

Her hair had been cut short, brushed back and styled elegantly against her head. She no longer felt any need to hide her face from the world, or anybody in it.

She had drawn a line between her past and her future, and her transformation had rocked him onto the back foot. If he hadn't known what to say to her before, he was totally at sea now.

He concentrated on practical business, contacting the firm she'd mentioned. A posse of dark-suited men descended from their offices in Milan, looked the *palazzo* over and expressed enthusiasm. There were discussions with Julia. How much could she invest? What value did she put on her restoration work? Finally they declared that they already had investors on their books eager for just such an opportunity.

They agreed to the idea of a Carnival party to make the press announcement, after which serious work would begin, to have everything ready for the following year.

When they'd gone Vincenzo walked around the empty building, trying to come to terms with the way his life had been turned upside down yet again, but this time in a manner that offered him new hope.

'To come back,' he murmured. 'To see it come alive again.'

'It'll be wonderful,' Julia said. She had been keeping a little behind him, in the shadows.

He looked at her, thinking that here was something else to unsettle him. He was just about growing used to her changed appearance.

She might have stepped out of the pages of *Vogue*. She was elegant, groomed to perfection, wearing a white silk shirt and the very latest fashionable trouser suit in dark blue. The perfume that reached him was as clear and subtle as a spring flower.

She belonged in a palace, he realised. The lost soul he'd first met had been an aberration. Now she was mistress of the situation, mistress of her own life at last. She exuded confidence from every pore, every sleekly groomed line. He could almost feel her being carried away from him by an irresistible current.

'I'm going to start work down here,' she said, indicating the great hall.

'I thought this was where we were having the press party.'

'It is. This will give us a point of interest to show people.'

'I see. Good idea.'

Would they ever, he wondered, have anything else to talk about but business?

Julia watched him standing at the foot of the great staircase, looking up.

What did he see? Perhaps it was his fiancée, the woman he had loved more than all the world, slowly descending, receiving the tribute of his radiant expression? Was this why he had suddenly become unable to draw closer to her?

'I'd better be going,' she said. 'Rosa knows something's up, and she wants to be told *everything*.'

He grinned. 'I can just hear her saying it.'

'Will you be in for supper tonight?'

'I'm afraid not. The tourists are already beginning to arrive for Carnival, and the restaurant is busy. We'll have to move fast if this place is going to be ready for the big evening.'

An army of cleaners moved in the following day. Julia took Rosa along to see them at work, and to keep a jealous eye on the frescoes.

'I'm going to set up work just here, behind the staircase,' she told her. 'I might even give a demonstration at the party.'

'Aren't you going to wear a beautiful dress?'

'If I'm going to paint, I'm probably better in jeans. But you can wear a beautiful dress. What about the one you told me about, the one your mother bought for you?'

'But aren't—you my mother?'

'Yes, darling, but she was too.'

Suddenly Julia remembered that Rosa had never wept for Bianca's death, and, perhaps, now she might feel that she never could. She hurried to say, 'You don't have to choose between us. It's all right to love us both.'

Rosa's eyes were wide with relief. 'Is it *really*?'

'Of course. You've got two mothers. She's *Mamma* and I'm Mummy. It's all very simple.'

She hugged the little girl and Rosa seemed happier, but Julia still had the feeling that something was being held back. Patience, she told herself.

The next moment Rosa startled her.

'When are you and Uncle Vincenzo going to get married?'

'I—what makes you think that we'll get married?'

'But you must. It would make everything perfect. He can't keep living in a hotel.'

How like a child, Julia thought, to see the matter in a sensible light. It was true that there were many realistic reasons for their marriage. And just as many reasons why it could never happen.

'It takes a little more than that,' she said carefully. 'People have to love each other as well.'

'But of course he loves you. Do you want me to ask him?'

'*No!*' Julia exploded before she could stop herself.

'All right,' Rosa said plaintively. 'I only thought—'

'Darling, do me a favour,' Julia begged. 'Stop thinking. Put it right out of your head.'

She thought she'd gained her point, but a moment later Rosa said, 'Is it Gina?'

'Who?'

'Gina, that he was going to marry. Everyone says he was dotty about her, but that was ages ago.'

'And everyone still talks about how she swept down that staircase and he looked at her adoringly,' Julia couldn't help saying. 'Even now, so long after.'

Rosa looked at her wisely.

'Perhaps you should make them talk about you,' she said.

For years afterwards, Julia wondered if she'd known, even then, what her daughter was planning. She denied it to herself, but sometimes even her own secrets were hidden from her.

Carnival started on February tenth, the first day of a two-and-a-half-week-long feast of gaiety and indulgence.

'Aaaa-aaah!' Julia greeted the day with a luxurious sigh up to the deep blue sky. 'This is gorgeous. I can't believe it's still so early in the year. Look at this weather.'

'The sun always comes out for Carnival,' Vincenzo told her, 'even if it goes in again afterwards.'

The festivities were everywhere. Outrageous costumes, topped by mysterious masks, could be seen whirling through the *piazzas* and peering around corners.

Harlequin and Columbine, Pantalone, Pulcinello, Pierrot, Pierrette: they all danced through the music-haunted streets, celebrating the wild liberty that came with anonymity.

Rosa seemed to have forgotten her resolve to play no part in the jollity, except that Julia sensed it was not so much forgotten as put aside for the moment. She now seemed determined to make Julia take her responsibilities as hostess seriously.

The party was to be in eighteenth century dress, and brilliant costumes began to appear in Julia's room, to be pored over, then returned to the hire shop. Rosa was ruthless about discarding any that did not appeal to her.

'But I rather like that gold one,' Julia said.

'The white one is better,' Rosa said firmly.

It was truly a glorious dress, satin and brocade, with a tiny waist. In a few minutes Julia was surveying herself in the mirror, adding yet one more persona to the long list she'd acquired recently.

She wasn't quite certain who this mysterious creature might be, with her sequinned gown and mask. But she felt it might be fun to be her for a while.

When the cleaners had finished work at the *palazzo* they were able to move into a few rooms temporarily, and oversee the arrangements. Over five hundred people would be there. Some were press, others had bought costly tickets. Venice was alive with rumours and nobody wanted to miss this event.

Even baby Carlo was brought to sleep there for a couple of nights, for no Venetian was ever too young for Carnival.

Acting on Rosa's instructions, Julia had not mentioned her costume to Vincenzo, who, as far as she knew, had made no plans to dress up.

'Shame on you,' she teased. 'You're the host of this party and you should be wearing satin knee breeches and lace.'

But she'd misjudged him. He was a Venetian, and satin and lace held no terrors for him. On the night he appeared before her in all his glory. Eighteenth-century garb suited him. The brocade of the black and gold coat and the lace at the neck had the strange effect of underlining his masculinity.

'Dressed like this,' he said, 'a rake could go out on the town and—' He broke off with a wistful, reminiscent sigh.

'Fine,' she told him. 'We'll go out on the town—but together.'

He might have answered, but Gemma looked in to say, 'Rosa has a surprise for you.' She vanished, leaving the door open.

After a moment Rosa appeared. She was wearing a pink satin carnival dress. It was grand and glorious, sweeping the floor, with sleeves like wings. On her head she wore a bonnet of pink satin and lace, and in her hand she held a pink, full-face mask on a stick.

Slowly she advanced towards them, the mask held up over her face, and sank down in an elegant curtsey. They all smiled and applauded, and she rose.

But she did not remove the mask, just stood there, her

shoulders seeming to sag. It was Julia who reached out
to draw the mask away, revealing that behind it the child
was in tears.

She didn't try to hide them now, just stood there with
them sliding down her cheeks.

'This is the dress you told me about?' she said.

Rosa nodded.

'*Mamma* bought it for me, for Carnival,' she said huskily. 'But I wouldn't wear it because I was angry with
her for going away. Now—' a sob shook her '—now I
want to tell her that I'm sorry, *and it's too late.*'

At last she could hold back no longer, and when Julia
opened her arms she went into them, weeping.

Julia held her close, torn between pain for her child
and happiness that Rosa had opened her heart to her.

'It's not too late,' she said. 'There's still a couple of
days of Carnival to go. Tomorrow we'll go to San
Michele together.'

'Can we really?' Rosa was transformed.

'Tonight everyone can see how lovely you look. And
tomorrow you can tell her all about it.'

'Can I wear my dress to San Michele, for *Mamma*?'

'Of course you can.' She dried the child's tears.

When Rosa had gone Julia glanced at Vincenzo who
had remained silent and very still, watching them. She
wished she could read the expression in his eyes, but his
jewelled mask concealed them.

'Aren't you going to get dressed?' he asked. 'I don't
even know what you're wearing yet.'

'Excellent. Then you won't know which one is me. I
think I'll enjoy that.'

'You'll drive me too far.'

'I probably will in the end, but we aren't nearly there

yet.' Her eyes dared him. 'It's going to be a fascinating journey.'

'Julia—'

'I think people are arriving. You'd better go and greet them.'

'What about you? This is as much your night as mine.'

'I'll be there.'

From the first moment the evening was a triumph. The knowledge that the Palazzo Montese was to live again had aroused interest all over Venice, throughout the hotel industry, and among those who passed their lives in one hotel after another.

Julia left the spotlight to Vincenzo, while she worked in the corner she had set apart for restoration, answering a stream of fascinated questions. She was dressed quietly and simply in velvet trousers and silk shirt.

Rosa was having the time of her life, but at last she came and fetched Julia determinedly, taking her hand and drawing her upstairs. Gemma was there, and the two of them helped her to dress.

'Time to go,' she said at last. 'This way.'

Brooking no argument, Rosa took her hand and led her down as far as the top of the main staircase.

'Darling, I don't think—'

'Go and stand in front of that picture, the one of Annina.'

Too dazed to do anything but obey, Julia went down to stand before the picture. Something drew her eyes up to the wild face of the woman who had once seemed so like herself in her misfortunes.

Not any more. It was time to do what Annina had never been able to do, to seize her fate and wrest it to her own will. An excitement was growing in her. She knew now why Rosa had done this.

Behind her she could hear the buzz of the crowd fall silent. Slowly she turned.

Vincenzo was standing at the foot of the steps, looking up at her. As she had always known he would be. As Rosa had always known he would be.

Slowly Julia began to descend, a vision in shimmering white, her face covered by a white lace mask. After a few steps she removed it, looking down on the man who never took his eyes from her.

His hand moved up to his own mask, seized it, tossed it away. Now she had a clear view of his face, and it was brilliant with love and happiness. It was the look she had longed to see.

He didn't take his eyes from her as she approached closer and closer. The masks were gone. Now there was only truth.

'Who—are you?' he asked uncertainly.

She was standing before him. Slowly she kissed him, then drew back at once.

'That's who I am,' she said. 'The woman who loves you.'

Once more she laid her lips on his, and kept them there while his hands settled on her waist, lifting her into the air, while not letting his mouth part from hers.

The crowd broke into applause, although none of them was really sure why. Somebody must have started it, but it could have been anyone. It might even have been a little girl, watching gleefully from above, determined to make this turn out right. A good organiser. Her mother's daughter.

There were still formalities to be gone through, guests to be greeted, smiles to give. But everything that happened now seemed part of a dream, and the only reality came at the end of the evening when Rosa led them to the side entrance, where a gondolier was waiting.

As they pulled away Vincenzo blew her a grateful kiss, before leaning back against the cushions, drawing Julia into his arms.

'I think it's all been taken out of our hands,' he said.

'Perhaps it's the only way it could happen,' she agreed. 'Why did everything suddenly become so hard?'

'A thousand times I came to the edge of telling you how much I love you, and want to marry you. But I became afraid in case you thought I was seizing you for fear of what I'd lose. I wanted you to trust me and I didn't think you ever would.'

'If you'd told me that you loved me, I'd have trusted and believed you,' she said fervently. 'And I could have said that I love you.'

'I wasn't sure that you did. You tried so often to warn me that you couldn't love me.'

'That was foolish of me. I love you with all my heart.'

'If you say that, I have nothing else to want. I know now that I was wrong. Not everyone leaves. I'm not going to *let* you leave me.'

He kissed her fiercely, letting his passion make the argument for him, feeling her response give him the answer that said more than speech.

'Are you sure it isn't a risk?' she murmured.

'Maybe. My risk.'

'*Our* risk.'

He nodded. 'Our risk. But love is always a risk, and I'll take it if you will.'

The gondola was leaving the centre of the city behind, leaving the music, the dancing and the wild figures, drifting into the semi darkness, where the little canals were illuminated only by tiny lamps and silence waited around every corner.

He took her hand in his, holding it tightly.

'If there is any safety in the world,' he said, looking at their clasped hands, 'it's here. But perhaps we shouldn't ask for safety, just a light showing the way to the next canal, and perhaps the one after that.'

She didn't answer in words, but when he released her hand and laid his lips on hers she gave herself up to him completely. All turmoil stilled. All questions answered.

Behind them the gondolier rowed silently, taking them towards the light that showed the way to the next canal, and the one after that, and then onward to wherever the future led.

MILLS & BOON®

Live the emotion

Tender
romance™

A FAMILY FOR KEEPS by Lucy Gordon (Heart to Heart)

Vincenzo saw that Julia had been to hell and back. It was up to
him to show her how wonderful the world could be. Julia never
thought she would laugh again…or kiss a gorgeous man. But she
did – with Vincenzo! Life was perfect – then Vincenzo made a
shocking discovery…

THE BUSINESS ARRANGEMENT by Natasha Oakley

For as long as Amy has known Hugh Balfour, she's loved him.
Her strategy was to avoid him at all costs – but now he needs a
PA…and only Amy will do! But he expects twenty-four-hour
attention – especially now he's looking at his old friend in a *very*
different light!

FIRST PRIZE: MARRIAGE by Jodi Dawson

When Dixie Osborn enters a competition to win a secluded
mountain lodge, she never expects to win! She's thrilled – but
there's a catch… Dixie's ticket was stuck to another – there's a
tie! Now she has to share the lodge with the totally gorgeous Jack
Powers for four days…

THE BLIND-DATE SURPRISE by Barbara Hannay
(Southern Cross)

The loneliness of the Outback is driving Annie McKinnon crazy.
How is a woman supposed to find love when the nearest eligible
man lives miles away? When she meets her dream man over the
Internet, she wants to dash to the city to meet him. But her blind
date has a secret…

On sale 4th March 2005

*Available at most branches of WHSmith, Tesco, ASDA, Martins,
Borders, Eason, Sainsbury's and all good paperback bookshops.*

Visit www.millsandboon.co.uk

EXtra

Favourite, award-winning or bestselling authors. Bigger reads, bonus short stories, new books or much-loved classics. *Always* **fabulous reading!**

Don't miss:

EXTRA passion for your money! (March 2005)
Emma Darcy – Mills & Boon Modern Romance
NEW *Mistress to a Tycoon* and **CLASSIC** *Jack's Baby*

EXTRA special for your money! (April 2005)
Sherryl Woods – Silhouette Special Edition –
Destiny Unleashed. This **BIG** book is about a woman
who is finally free to choose her own path…love,
business or a little sweet revenge?

EXTRA tender for your money! (April 2005)
Betty Neels & Liz Fielding – Mills & Boon
Tender Romance – **CLASSIC** *The Doubtful Marriage*
and **BONUS,** *Secret Wedding*
Two very popular writers write two very different,
emotional stories on the always-bestselling wedding theme.

Available at most branches of WHSmith, Tesco, ASDA, Martins, Borders, Eason, Sainsbury's and all good paperback bookshops.

www.silhouette.co.uk

0305/154

FREE!

4 Books
and a surprise gift!

We would like to take this opportunity to thank you for reading this Mills & Boon® book by offering you the chance to take FOUR more specially selected titles from the Tender Romance™ series absolutely FREE! We're also making this offer to introduce you to the benefits of the Reader Service™—

- ★ **FREE home delivery**
- ★ **FREE gifts and competitions**
- ★ **FREE monthly Newsletter**
- ★ **Exclusive Reader Service offers**
- ★ **Books available before they're in the shops**

Accepting these FREE books and gift places you under no obligation to buy, you may cancel at any time, even after receiving your free shipment. Simply complete your details below and return the entire page to the address below. You don't even need a stamp!

YES! Please send me 4 free Tender Romance books and a surprise gift. I understand that unless you hear from me. I will receive 6 superb new titles every month for just £2.75 each, postage and packing free. I am under no obligation to purchase any books and may cancel my subscription at any time. The free books and gift will be mine to keep in any case.

N5ZEF

Ms/Mrs/Miss/Mr ....Initials.................................

BLOCK CAPITALS PLEASE

Surname ....

Address...

....Postcode ....

Send this whole page to:
UK: FREEPOST CN8I, Croydon, CR9 3WZ